MILLSTONE MURDERS

BUT WHOEVER CAUSES ONE OF THESE LITTLE
ONES WHO BELIEVE IN ME TO SIN

THOMAS DI NUNZIO

Copyright © 2025 by Thomas Di Nunzio.

All rights reserved.

No portion of this book may be reproduced in any form without written permission from the publisher or author, except as permitted by U.S. copyright law.

Printed in the United States of America

Disclaimer: The author and publisher make no representations or warranties with respect to the accuracy or completeness of the contents of this work and specifically disclaim all warranties, including without limitation warranties of fitness for a particular purpose. No warranty may be created or extended by sales or promotional materials. The advice and strategies contained herein may not be suitable for every situation. This work is sold with the understanding that the author and publisher are not engaged in rendering legal, accounting, or other professional services. If professional assistance is required, the services of a competent professional person should be sought.

Library of Congress Reg. # 2025919061

Cover Design by: Authors Hike

Publisher: Authors Hike

For permission requests, please contact: srv1841@aol.com

Dedication

To the children

who were betrayed, silenced,

and scarred by those they trusted.

May this story honor your strength,

shine a light on hidden darkness,

and remind the world that your voices are heard.

About the Author

Thomas Di Nunzio spent over 25 years in law enforcement, rising to captain while hunting predators and confronting the darkest corners of society. Now retired, he channels that relentless pursuit of truth into mystery, crime, and psychological thrillers. Gritty, uncompromising and steeped in real-world insight, his stories drag readers into shadows where justice is messy, evil wears many faces and survival often comes at a cost.

Table of Contents

Chapter 1

Leaning against the wall among a line of uniformed boys stood a 13-year-old with dark hair and striking blue eyes. He wore the same outfit as the rest, white shirt, blue tie, blue pants, but there was a casual tilt to his stance, one loafer pressed against the wall behind him, that made it look like he owned the place. His crooked smile gave off an air of cocky confidence, and the other kids noticed. So did the teachers.

But the truth about him ran deeper.

Despite appearances, he wasn't a troublemaker. Kind by nature and respectful to his elders, he was the type of kid who'd hold open a door or step aside without being asked. But if you pushed him, if you crossed a line, he didn't hesitate to push back. Hard. Consequences be damned.

That was something his father had drilled into him early on.

This was Dominic Di Angelo.

The schoolyard at St. Magnus stretched wide, its blacktop shimmering under the early morning sun. A ten-foot aluminum cross loomed above the yard, mounted proudly on the beige-brick face of the school building. Beside it, bold aluminum letters spelled out: *St. Magnus.* Below the cross, clusters of seventh and eighth-graders idled. The girls huddled in tight little circles, whispering into one another's ears. The boys tossed a scuffed tennis ball against the wall, their laughter punctuated by the rhythmic thud of the rubber ball on the brick.

From a distance, the blacktop sparkled with millions of glittering specks, harmless-looking, but mostly the remnants of shattered bottles. They caught the light like gemstones, a quiet reminder that this was the slightly rougher side of town.

Dominic had entered St. Magnus in the fourth grade. That was when his world, and his family, began to splinter.

He'd been just eight years old when his mother died. A third grader in the local public school, too young to fully grasp the permanence of loss, but old enough to feel it in every empty seat, every missed lunch, every school trip or PTA meeting where other kids had someone cheering them on.

His father, Jimmy, devastated by the loss of his young wife, did his best to hold the line. But the Di Angelo family had gone from three to two, and there were some cracks in their foundation that just couldn't be filled.

They lived in a modest brick home on Merchant Street in Pennsauken, New Jersey. Jimmy was a good father, hardworking and proud, but the local public schools weren't equipped to support a kid like Dominic. Not that he needed special attention. But he needed somewhere to go after school while Jimmy was working.

There were no after-school programs, no real safety net offered by the public schools, and Jimmy's younger sister, Gia, was busy working toward a degree in veterinary medicine. It was demanding, and Jimmy didn't want her to fall behind or lose her scholarship by slipping below the required GPA. So, he did his best not to burden her, although, more often than not, she was his only option. Dominic loved being with her. Still, it was complicated.

Jimmy wanted to raise his son with a solid foundation, to teach him values and traditions, some he had grown up with, and others he wished he had. He tried. He even made an effort to get them to Sunday Mass once in a while, though work or exhaustion usually got in the way. Most nights, he had to lesave Dominic with Gia or a neighbor for a few hours.

Bartending at his cousin's bar, *The Philly Tavern*, wasn't glamorous, but it was steady. And Jimmy wasn't the type to let family down by showing up late or missing a shift. Between that job and a modest disability pension, it was just enough to keep things going. He was grateful for the work, and he showed it by being dependable. So dependable, in fact, that most patrons assumed he owned the place.

Everyone called him "Jimmy D."

One night at the Tavern, an elderly man slid onto a stool and asked for a Macallan, neat. Jimmy sized him up with the instinct of a seasoned bartender and poured the drink without a word. One neat Scotch turned into three, and over the course of the evening, the two men really got to know each other.

The man was sharp, seated, insightful, with a quiet confidence that spoke of a life well lived. Jimmy picked up on it right away. The kind of guy who didn't need to prove he was smart, he just was. Their conversation ranged from faith and family to politics and finances. Nothing was off the table.

The man listened closely, and when Jimmy spoke about Dominic and the struggle to balance work and parenting, he was sympathetic. Before leaving the bar that night, he introduced himself properly:

Monsignor Michael Cipolla. Of St. Magnus.

Then came the offer, free tuition for Dominic at St. Magnus, with after-school care included. Jimmy was stunned. His first thought was that maybe the priest had knocked back one too many Macallans. But the Monsignor wasn't drunk.

A few days later, after careful thought, Jimmy met with Cipolla again. They talked, made arrangements, and by the end of the meeting, it was settled: Dominic would start at St. Magnus in the fall. Tuition waived. After-school supervision is taken care of.

It was a blessing.

Jimmy truly believed he was doing right by his son. But nothing ever comes without a cost.

A few years after Dominic started at St. Magnus, Monsignor Cipolla retired. When Jimmy asked whether the new guy would be anything like him, easy to talk to, down to earth, the Monsignor just shrugged and said, "Probably not, Jimmy D."

Sure enough, a few months later, his replacement arrived. The new priest was cold, distant, and, worst of all, not even Italian. That bothered Jimmy more than anything on the man's résumé. However, if you were a priest, a garbageman or an ambassador, it didn't matter. Two guys talking over a Scotch and sharing a bowl of stale peanuts, that was a bond in Jimmy's eyes. Unless you were in the military, titles didn't mean a damn thing to Jimmy.

Now in his final year at St. Magnus, Dominic had long since realized that kids in Catholic school could be just as rough as the ones in public school, maybe worse. St. Magnus was no exception.

Sure, they wore ties and recited prayers, but once they hit the schoolyard, it was all clenched fists and sharp tongues. Dominic learned fast that Catholic school didn't make you a better Christian. Other than the first-period Religion class, it didn't mean a damn thing once the final bell rang and the classroom doors swung open.

Out in the yard, the commandments didn't carry weight, not when fists flew. The Good News Bible stayed tucked inside those gray laminated flip-top desks. Sundays were for show. Neat hair, clean shoes. No sneakers. That's when the commandments were back in play. But come Monday morning, the same altar boys who rang bells and swung incense turned back into kids who'd knock you flat for looking at them the wrong way.

Sunday Mass lasted forty-five minutes on average. That's how long most St. Magnus boys, and a few of the girls, held onto their Christianity. Maybe less if you only attended or served at the Saturday 4:00 p.m., vigil. Serving Mass made you feel like you were one of the good ones, even if it was just for a day.

It didn't take long for Dominic's reputation to settle in.

"He ain't afraid to throw down with anyone," they'd whisper, sometimes in awe, sometimes in warning, depending on the crowd.

And it was true. Dominic never went looking for a fight, but he never backed down from one either.

That was Jimmy's influence. His father had a presence about him, sharp-looking, always in neatly pressed shirts, clean-shaven, with piercing blue eyes that cut through people. He was old school. The kind of man who believed that if someone put their hands on you, you put them down twice as hard.

"Nobody's gonna hand you respect, Dom. You take it, or you don't get it at all."

That was Jimmy's mantra. Dominic absorbed it like the gospel. By the time he was ten, his fists already knew what they were doing, and his heart beat a little faster when things got tense. Respect came not because he asked for it, but because he demanded it, quietly, and when necessary, with blood.

"Help the weaker kids, and don't let the bullies push you around, or when you get home, I'll push you around." Another one of his father's mantras.

Dominic wasn't afraid of his father. To outsiders, Jimmy looked rough and tough, the six-foot Marine vet who carried himself like a man you didn't want to mess with. But Dominic knew better. His father wasn't about hitting his kid, so nobody else had better either.

They had a bond stronger than anything. Dominic adored him, and Jimmy loved his son more than anything else in this world. It was all they really had.

Those words, *Help the weaker...*, stuck. Over time, they stopped sounding like fatherly advice and started to feel like a commandment. Maybe even divine instruction. Somewhere deep inside, Dominic came to believe that God Himself had entrusted him with that mission: to *protect the weak.*

Good thing he didn't mind fighting.

It seemed like for every tough kid at St. Magnus, there was a quiet one being picked on. Every single day.

The morning schoolyard bell rang at exactly 8:00 a.m., sharp and piercing. Conversations cut off mid-sentence. Kids scrambled into formation, four neat lines, just like they'd practiced. The chaos of the yard dissolved under the watchful gaze of a small, wiry nun. Sister Jean.

She stood no taller than five feet, her face etched with decades of discipline and devotion. A silver wisp of hair peeked out from beneath her starched black habit, and her thick, black-framed glasses never slipped, not even when she turned her head with the sharp precision of a drill sergeant.

She didn't need to shout. Her voice, low and firm, carried the kind of authority that comes from years of experience in the classroom. The students respected her. Feared her a little, too. She knew all their names.

Adjusting her glasses, she began the morning roll call, calling students by formal titles, "Master" for boys, "Miss" for girls, with a tone that was somehow both gentle and commanding. The lines peeled away one by one, each group heading toward classrooms labeled 7A through 8B.

Inside, the boy with the blue eyes took his seat near the middle of the room, surrounded by familiar faces. A low hum of conversation buzzed across the rows of desks. The day officially began after the morning prayer and the Pledge of Allegiance.

First class: Religion.

Then the classroom door opened.

A thin, slight man entered, dressed in a black shirt and clerical collar. His gold-framed glasses caught the morning light. Behind him, scrawled in white chalk on the slate-black board, were the words:

Current Events

Kent State Shooting

Beside it, a hand-drawn peace sign.

He didn't inspire the children.

He didn't have the look or the presence to stir young minds. Nothing about him said *apostle* or *holy man*. He was scrawny, with thinning, oily hair and small, stained teeth. There was an odour, too, something stale and sour that clung to him. The kids had hoped for someone else. Someone cooler. Someone who walked in with a warm smile and wavy hair that just brushed his collar, maybe a bit of stubble like the pictures of Jesus taped to the classroom walls. Someone who sat on the edge of a desk and talked about life like he'd actually lived it.

Instead, they got Asher.

Father Bernard Asher.

He showed no signs that he'd ever lived life like the parents of the children sitting before him. He didn't look athletic. He didn't look like he'd ever kissed a girl, swung a hammer, turned a screwdriver, or been popular, ever. Maybe that was part of it. Become a priest. Wrap yourself in the title. Gain some kind of authority over people who, without the collar and robes, wouldn't give you a second look.

When Father Asher entered a room, the air didn't lighten; it curdled. You could feel it in your chest. Not panic, but something close. A quiet pressure that made you sit straighter, speak softer, want to disappear.

And the sermons, God, the sermons, were worse.

Dry, muttered words with too many stops and starts, as if he wasn't sure what to say or didn't believe it himself. His homilies droned on about sin and obedience, never about love or forgiveness, never about hope. Most of the kids tuned out within the first few minutes. They stared through him, past him, praying for the bell. Wishing instead for the crumple of brown paper lunch bags from lockers, or the comforting scent of cafeteria food, especially on pizza day. Anything but Asher's voice, thick with stale cologne, cigarettes, and bad coffee.

The students didn't fear him like they feared nuns with rulers or teachers with tempers. This was different. An unease they couldn't quite put a name to.

Without waiting for silence, Father Asher launched into a booming lecture. He was already pacing in front of the room, gesturing with sudden bursts of energy.

He spoke about Jesus washing the feet of His disciples.

"A call for trust!" he declared. His voice echoed down the hallway through the open door.

Dominic caught fragments of it.

"Not just as a divine act, but as a human one. A gesture of humility," Asher continued, his voice growing more impassioned.

Dominic was only half-listening, but something about the phrase stuck with him. *A call for trust.*

Father Asher raised his voice. "We will reenact this scene! I will play the part of Jesus. You will be my Apostles. Twelve volunteers."

Extra credit, he added.

Extra credit! I could absolutely use extra credit, Dominic thought.

The room erupted.

Hands flew into the air. Voices overlapped.

"Girls, too?"

"Can I be Jesus?"

"Can we wear flip-flops?"

"Do I have to take off my socks?"

Father Asher flushed red. He raised a hand for silence.

"No flip-flops," he said sharply. "Bare feet."

His eyes swept the room.

"If no one volunteers, I will choose twelve of you, six boys and six girls, myself. You are the Apostles. I am Jesus. Now open your *Good News Bibles* to John, chapter thirteen."

Chapter 2

Current Day

A narrow street stretched ahead of the tactical vehicles, their lights dimmed but engines humming quietly in the early dawn. A bulky van, marked **"High Tech Crimes Unit Task Force – Mobile Lab," idled a block away, its pale blue light spilling from the** interior.

Captain Di Angelo stood with one foot planted on the pavement, the other resting on the step of his Ford Explorer. The driver's side door hung open behind him. Dressed head to toe in black tactical gear, his Kevlar vest was tight across his chest, the radio on his shoulder crackling faintly. With his left hand, he reached across his chest, fingers curling around the mic strapped to his right shoulder, ready to squeeze the call button. Lips pressed tight to the receiver, he hovered in the moment, poised, tense, seconds away from issuing the *"hit"* command.

A command that was about to change lives.

Some for the better.

But for at least one person, not so much.

The specialized High Tech Crimes Task Force, a coalition of ICE agents, U.S. Marshals, State Police, and local detectives, moved with precision. Their black uniforms and body armor blended into the shadows. *TASK FORCE* was emblazoned across the backs of their vests; the fronts simply read *POLICE.* Their mission was clear: to target the sickest of criminals. Their prey: child predators, child pornographers, and pedophiles.

Captain Di Angelo had spearheaded the creation of the task force after a chance discovery years earlier.

Back when he was still a sergeant in the Narcotics Undercover Division, he'd stumbled across a forgotten box of unopened envelopes marked *ICAC* in the Tech Support Unit.

That unit was supposed to dump data from cell phones for investigations, assist with wiretaps, and install surveillance cameras to monitor drug deals and gang activity within Camden City and several counties within New Jersey. When Di Angelo asked the Tech Unit sergeant what **"ICAC"** meant, the man had muttered, "Internet Crimes against Children."

"What's in the envelopes?" He asked the sergeant of that unit.

"You don't want to know, Di Angelo. You don't want to get involved."

But Di Angelo did get involved. He opened one envelope, and then another, and another, until he felt sick to his stomach. Inside each envelope was a disc. Thirty discs in all from that box. Some were over a year old. All full of child pornography. Case after case, handed to the office in a wrapped box and bow. All the office had to do was follow up. It should've been acted on immediately. The signs were there, obvious, rotting at the edges. But for some reason, it wasn't. Maybe the system was blind. Maybe it chose to be.

In his years with the county, Di Angelo had worked in several units. He was pulled in multiple directions because he got results.

He started as a patrol officer, chasing criminals through the city, getting shot at more than once. He'd been hit once, badly enough that he could've taken early retirement.

But that wasn't his style.

He moved on to Homicide, pulling twenty-hour shifts, growing a beard, keeping his hair long for deep undercover operations, and living under false identities for months at a time. He took pride in all of it. The work was brutal, but nobody begged him to be a cop.

He *wanted* it. He *loved* it. It gave him purpose. It gave him results.

But nothing, not a single bust, not even the most high-profile conviction, ever felt as urgent as the cases that had been sitting in that forgotten box on a shelf, collecting dust.

He believed God had led him to it. He truly did.

"These poor victims," he thought.

The victims no one else wanted to see. The ones too small, too broken, too silenced.

The crimes in that cardboard box weren't like the ones Di Angelo or the rest of the office were used to seeing. These were different. These were *damnations*, hiding in plain sight.

He knew he had to do something.

He wasn't going to let this rot away in silence. He was going to create a unit, at the very least, a task force. Not just another initiative or pilot program, but a dedicated team with teeth. With reach. One capable of breaking into the hidden world of deviant sexual crimes festering behind screens and encrypted devices.

He didn't know *how* yet, but he knew he'd figure it out.

It already felt more important than any case he'd ever worked.

Because this wasn't about headlines, it wasn't about arrest stats or televised press conferences.

This was about a debt.

One that started long ago, inside the stone walls of St. Magnus. An itch that never quite went away.

The County Police Chief and the sergeant, two men sworn to uphold the law, had known exactly what they were looking at. A digital purgatory of evidence. And they'd done nothing.

When Di Angelo brought his findings to Commissioner Mary Scola, his voice cracked, not from emotion, but from the pressure of holding in his fury.

"They should be charged," he said, low and sharp. "They should be charged with dereliction of duty. For every day they let that filth sit unchallenged. For every kid who got hurt while sitting on their hands. They're complicit."

Mary Scola didn't argue.

She *couldn't.*

The numbers were brutal.

She assured him she would look into the matter and back him if there was pushback.

He didn't wait.

He began investigating on his own, placing calls to ICAC, the Internet Crimes Against Children program that had originally provided the leads. On the other end of the line, they were shocked. Someone was *finally* returning their calls.

They explained what was needed: digital intelligence tools, state-of-the-art systems to trace online activity, identify predators, and track the sharing of illegal content.

With their help, and after a year of relentless lobbying and political arm-twisting, the High-Tech Crimes Task Force finally got the funding it needed.

Mary kept her word.

Most of it.

The so-called powers that be didn't give a damn about protecting kids.

That much had become clear to Di Angelo after years of watching the machine grind away. What they cared about was protecting their own public image. Their reputations. Their pensions. Their clean, polished press conferences, where they could pretend they were doing something meaningful.

Di Angelo knew the game. And he played along.

Whatever it took to get them to open the coffers.

If it had been about helping their own, governors, congressmen, and police chiefs, the money would've poured in. But kids? Victims? They didn't move the needle. Not until whispers of child predators living in quiet neighborhoods, hundreds of child pornographers hiding in plain sight within their own congressional districts, began to leak to the press.

Then, suddenly, everyone wanted to look like a hero.

To save face.

Not their souls.

Not because they cared.

Naturally, there was a catch. There's *always* a catch.

If the unit, and all its expensive tech, drones, and gleaming black government-issued vehicles, didn't meet its "quota," they'd pull the plug. Shut it down like a failed investment, like it hadn't been the only lifeline for the most vulnerable: innocent children.

That was the game.

It didn't matter that they were chasing monsters who traded in children's pain. What mattered to the brass were numbers, arrests, search warrants, overtime hours, and fiscal quarters. They wanted statistics, not justice.

At some point, New Jersey politicians had sold their souls to the devil. The problem was that no one could remember exactly when the corruption had taken root. It had just crept in, quiet, steady, devouring the good from the inside out.

The good guys, what few were left, were just hanging on. Clutching at whatever scraps of morality they still had.

And for Di Angelo, saving children felt like a good place to start.

"Help the weaker kid."

His father's voice still echoed in his mind, sharp and clear, like it had been carved into his bones. It wasn't just advice, it was a command. A code to live by.

Help the weaker kid.

And now, years later, standing at the helm of a task force built to hunt monsters, he knew he was still following that same rule.

***

This morning's target lived in a Cape Cod-style house with white siding, two dormers, and a black asphalt-shingled roof. The street was wide, with most cars parked in long driveways. White vinyl fences bordered many of the lawns, more for show than privacy.

It looked more like a community than a neighborhood. Cookie-cutter homes in different shades. The kind of place where people shoveled their own walks and grilled burgers by kidney-shaped pools surrounded by a few Adirondack chairs.

It wasn't filthy rich, but it wasn't poor either.

Mostly working-class. Unassuming.

A community of small business owners and people who'd worked their whole lives for a pension.

Dreams were simple on streets like this, Dreaming of the day they could sleep past 7 a.m., and watch their grandchildren play soccer on the weekends. Honest dreams. Modest ones. Just a little peace after a lifetime of hard work, in a quiet neighborhood, among neighbors who still waved from their driveways.

But today, peace was shattered at 1107 Greentree Road, the residence of Allen Hanlon. His house had the honor of today's search warrant.

Hanlon wasn't just some random name from a database. He had deep, rotting roots in the county's political circles. His brother, James Hanlon, sat high on the Supreme Court bench. Everyone either knew or strongly suspected that James had shielded his brother from numerous allegations over the years. But even this… even this crossed a line, even for a crooked judge.

When Di Angelo saw Allen Hanlon's name come through as the primary target in the child pornography case, he kept his mouth shut. He didn't loop in the chief. Not the prosecutor. Not even the commissioner. Weekly warrants had become routine now; no one looked twice. The chief didn't even ask questions anymore; each arrest was another pat on the back, another press release. Rinse and repeat.

Di Angelo couldn't care less. Unless the FBI came sniffing around, of course, trying to poach a high-profile case to pad their own bloated stats. He'd dealt with their type before. They liked easy wins, clean cases with straightforward paperwork, and perps too dumb to lawyer up.

Di Angelo caught on fast. He started "dirtying up" the cases just enough, dropping hints to the agents that there were too many moving parts, too many loose ends. They'd back off every time. Worked like a charm. Di Angelo even had a system for getting his search warrant signed, a method he drilled into his detectives like gospel. **Step One:** Know your judges. Know the ones who rubber-stamped paperwork without blinking. The lazy ones. Those who skimmed the probable cause and moved the pen.

Step Two: Timing was everything. Friday afternoons were gold. By then, the courthouse halls were hollow echoes, and the judges were already halfway down the Parkway in their minds, dreaming of cocktails, seaside decks, and whatever poor waitress they'd harass next.

Step Three: Play the game. Go old school. Bring two of your best-looking detectives. Make introductions. Smile. Small talk. Laugh at the judge's dumb jokes if you have to.

Di Angelo didn't respect most of them anyway. They were part of the same broken machine: introverts, perverts, and cowards. The only difference? Better suits.

Now, back in the present, the operation was live.

The comms buzzed in his earpiece.

"McKeown, Cap. In position. Ready on your go."

Di Angelo didn't hesitate.

"Received. Give it a soft knock."

A few measured raps on the front door echoed through the quiet street like kettle drums. Then silence.

A beat passed.

McKeown's voice returned, low, calm, and steady.

"Negative response, Cap."

The two men locked eyes across the lawn, each in the other's line of sight. The scene was familiar, almost choreographed like actors in a Broadway play performing night after night: same cues, same reactions, same finale. But improvisation was always welcome.

Di Angelo snapped the radio back onto his vest and raised his hand. McKeown spotted the signal and exhaled a soft, nasal chuckle.

"Get ready, guys," he said quietly.

He knew exactly what the gesture meant.

When Di Angelo's hand dropped, the game began.

The battering ram struck the door with a hollow boom, splintering the frame inward under the force of practiced urgency. Shouts followed, sharp, commanding, and unmistakable.

"Police! Search warrant!"

Boots thundered through the narrow hallway. The fragile entryway was gone, reduced to shattered trim and broken locks. And the sins hidden inside were about to be dragged into the cold light of morning.

Inside, just as they'd briefed, four people. Two adults. Two young girls. With any luck, the target would fess up early, sparing some shame and trauma for the rest of the household. Just show us. Tell us. Come with us. That's all it took.

Except, it's never that simple.

Raids like this didn't just catch criminals. They shattered families. They pulled secrets out of the shadows, secrets the predators prayed would stay buried, especially from the people sleeping down the hall. A seasoned detective learns to spot the difference. The innocent wear fear in their eyes. The guilty? They pretend at innocence, but behind their calm, it's there. You can feel it. A quiet, suffocating dread. The dread of damnation.

The Hanlon search warrant, although signed with relative ease, was going to be a different story. Di Angelo knew that once the news got hold of the fact that the brother of a Supreme Court judge was involved in a child pornography investigation and a search warrant was executed on his brother's house, the press was going to have a field day. Di Angelo was going to play dumb, but was ready to take the heat. It was worth it.

Inside, the team moved quickly through the house. The rooms were dark, shades drawn. Their weapon-mounted lights scanned the walls and floors in sharp sweeps.

"Police! Search warrant!"

The command echoed off drywall and hardwood. In the master bedroom, Allen Hanlon stood frozen by the bed, wearing nothing but white jockeys, his body shaking, eyes wide with confusion. Before he could move, officers had him face down on the floor, knees in his back. His wrists were zip-tied in seconds.

Detective Roberts knelt beside him, voice low and steady in Allen's ear.

"We have a search warrant for your home, Mr. Hanlon." He held the paperwork in his hand, angled so Hanlon could see. "Can you guess why we're here? I think you know exactly why."

Hanlon's voice cracked. "Can I speak to you privately, sir? I believe I do know why you're here."

From the bed, Dawn Hanlon shrieked, sitting up beneath the covers.

"Where are my girls? Girls! Mommy is here! Everything is okay!" she cried out, panic blooming in her voice.

Down the hall, two children, one seven, the other five, were curled up together in a single bed, the older girl clutching her sister protectively. Two female detectives entered gently, speaking in soft, steady tones as they led the girls downstairs to their mother, who now sat on the living room sofa, her hands zip-tied in front of her.

In a separate room, Allen sat across from the detectives, his demeanor passive, almost defeated. He didn't resist. He didn't deny. He admitted he'd seen "stuff" on his computer and voluntarily pointed them toward both his laptop and cell phone.

"I… I didn't search for anything illegal," he stammered, eyes darting. "It just… popped up! Some shit just pops up, you know?"

Detective Roberts stared at him, unblinking.

"Why don't you tell me what you *were* searching for, Mr. Hanlon?"

"You know… p-p-porn," Allen said, his voice barely above a whisper, trembling with shame and fear.

"Girls?" Roberts shot back.

A pause.

"You mean *little* girls. *Young* little girls. Not just 'girls.' Children. Children like the age of your own kids. Right?"

Allen opened his mouth, but nothing came out.

"Did you ever take pics of your daughters?" Roberts added offhandedly, like it had just occurred to him. "You did, didn't you?"

Roberts was doing a great job of pissing off Allen. That was his job. Be the prick cop who knew everything about the potential defendant, what he was thinking. What he was hiding. Giving the impression that the entry team had been surveilling him for months. Let him start to believe Roberts knew every key he ever stroked on his hidden laptop. Every sight he ever viewed. Most importantly, answer the questions being asked before the target had time to think of some bullshit answer on his own or before he lawyered up. Roberts and Di Angelo both knew he'd lawyer up soon. They knew who his brother was. So they pushed. Hard. Maybe they'd piss him off enough to say something stupid. Incriminating.

"No!" Allen finally shouted, twisting in his seat. "Please, my wife and kids can hear you! I'm sorry, Dawn! There's been a mistake, sweetie. They're wrong, honey! I didn't do anything! I need to call my attorney!"

Then he snapped, voice rising. "Do you know who my brother is?! I know powerful people. Your career as a cop is over, dude!"

Roberts didn't flinch.

"We called your brother."

It was a lie. But cops were allowed to lie, especially to predators like this.

Roberts lied a lot in child exploitation cases. The truth was already in the digital evidence. That was the beauty of these investigations, a perfect trail of virtual breadcrumbs, IP address to IP address, leading right to a very real, very tangible monster.

Across the room, Dawn Hanlon stood frozen, staring at the floor like it might crack open and swallow her whole. Her breath was shallow. Her lips barely moved.

She'd known Allen since high school. They lived just a few houses apart. He was older, old enough, in hindsight, that it was clear he'd started grooming her before she even knew what grooming was.

Allen worked in the Ironworkers Union, the same as her older brother, TJ. But unlike TJ, who'd earned his position through real skill and certified trade, Allen had always gotten in through the back door. Shady connections. Favors. Slipped resumes. Quiet nods in dark rooms.

With Allen, it was a gift job, nothing earned, all connections. He and TJ carpooled occasionally, though TJ hated him. As soon as TJ could afford his own car, he cut Allen off without a second thought.

Allen had weaseled his way into Dawn's life not long after TJ moved to Florida, taking full advantage of his absence. Dawn, young and gullible, fell for his game. He got her pregnant when she was just eighteen. Her acceptance to Rutgers quickly faded into the background, disappointing her parents and TJ tremendously. Her college dreams ended before they began. That's when life, the hard, unrelenting kind, started. She had no backup plan.

Allen, a bullshit artist with a gift for manipulation and just enough shady ties to seem important, became her entire world by default. Eventually, he greased his way into Crown Financial, a brokerage house steeped in backdoor deals. It wasn't just a job; it was a front. A laundering hub used by his brother and their crew of polished predators to move dark money, especially during election season.

Allen was the stooge, weak-willed, easily led, and secretly drowning in a child pornography addiction. He'd do anything they asked: pressure small businesses under contract to buy outlandish fundraiser tickets or risk losing their deals, bury scandals before they reached the press, and play the loyal errand boy. His brother, James Hanlon, was no cleaner.

James, a former high-priced defense attorney, had built his career in the shadows of monumental law firms, first as a junior associate grinding through motions, then as a courtroom strategist for clients who could afford to bury the truth under legal policy, no matter how unscrupulous it seemed. Eventually, he made partner at a firm crowded with former prosecutors, men and women who once claimed to serve justice, but now served power, influence, and salaries so substantial that they could keep their ears shut and their consciences clean.

James played both sides of the aisle. He whispered in judges' ears, manipulated plea deals, and shaped outcomes with surgical precision. When he was appointed to the State Supreme Court, his position helped grease the wheels for a string of favorable rulings, verdicts that raised eyebrows but never triggered formal inquiries. For those in the know, having Hanlon on the bench was like holding a master key to the justice system. Suspicious rulings and questionable decisions consistently benefited the wealthy defendant or buried the poor victim, just trying to find justice or any closure at all.

Having Hanlon on the bench was like playing three-card monte at a carnival. The game was rigged, and James not only supplied the deck but was also the dealer. His reputation was known among prosecutors, but the party in power looked the other way. His seat remained secure.

Allen Hanlon was much the same, just without the scrutiny of the public eye. His reputation wasn't spotless, though. There were whispers of insider trading, misused funds, and deals that reeked of corruption. And in certain private circles, Allen's dark proclivity for young girls was no secret, especially not to his brother. The powerful James Hanlon covered for Allen, the pawn. Dirty secrets hidden behind a judge's black robe and official title.

Di Angelo, along with others close to the front, knew all of this too.

As the scene unfolded in front of her, Dawn broke down. Her voice cracked, eyes brimming with panic and disbelief. "What did you do, Allen?!" she screamed, her breath catching in her throat. "What is going on?! Will someone please tell me what the hell is happening?"

She turned to the officers, her voice rising in desperation.

"My children, my children are going to need therapy after this, for God's sake! Allen!"

This wasn't how she pictured her life unraveling. If anything, she'd expected racketeering, laundering, some kind of white-collar crime Allen had gotten tangled in. She had almost expected it. A scandal, sure. But not *this*. Not a team of what looked to her like guerrilla fighters bursting into her home at five in the morning.

She sat on the sofa, zip-tied, trembling, clutching her daughters as best she could while armed strangers tore through drawers, closets, even her underwear. Her heart thundered in her chest. She felt exposed, powerless, and most of all, betrayed. She looked at Allen, waiting for him to say something. *Anything.* But his silence told her more than words ever could.

Sobbing hysterically, her older daughter leaned in close, her voice barely a whisper through the chaos.

"I'm sorry, Mommy," she cried. "It's my fault, Daddy's in trouble! I didn't tell them! I didn't tell them, Daddy!"

The little girl buried her face in Dawn's chest, her voice muffled by panic.

Dawn's blood ran cold.

"What, honey?" she asked, turning sharply, her breath catching.

She gathered her daughter into her arms, the younger one already curled into her lap. Both were now enclosed in the stronghold of her embrace, as if she were shielding them from an oncoming tornado. Perhaps she was. Her zip-tied wrists bit into her skin, deep red marks forming, but she didn't care.

All three had the same shade of blonde hair, their heads indistinguishable in the tight, trembling huddle, three halos of gold pressed together like a single, fragile knot.

Dawn's heart stopped with every sob.

"Tell me, honey," she said gently, trying to steady her voice. "What did you do to get Daddy in trouble?"

She tried to sound calm, like "everyday Mommy," even as her world shattered around her.

The seven-year-old struggled to find the words, to explain to her mother what Daddy had made her promise never to tell. She opened her mouth, tried to speak, but the words wouldn't come. They stayed lodged in her throat. She glanced toward her father, hoping for something, reassurance, maybe, but found nothing. Finally, she gave up, her small shoulders shaking as she buried her face in Dawn's chest and sobbed.

"It's okay, honey," Dawn whispered, stroking her daughter's golden hair with trembling fingers. "You don't have to say it. Mommy's here."

It was in that moment, wrapped in the warmth of her children, zip ties digging into her skin, that Dawn understood everything had changed. Life as she knew it was gone. She would have to summon a strength she wasn't sure she had. Raise them on her own. Face the shame, the whispers, the judgment. She had lost her family for marrying Allen, and now she would lose whatever illusion was left of the man she thought she knew. But none of that mattered as much as the little girl sobbing in her arms. Whatever damage Allen had done, Dawn would have to undo it, piece by piece. No matter how long it took. No matter where they had to go. Just as long as Allen wasn't there.

The house was still swarming with officers, dipping in and out of rooms, moving like dark shadows. The air crackled with radio transmissions and officers yelling, "clear" every so often. But in that moment, all Dawn could concentrate on was her daughter's cry, the fear in her eyes. The three were trembling. Captain Di Angelo entered the house, flanked by two High-Tech Crimes Unit (HTCU) detectives, unrecognizable from the entry team as they all wore the same uniform, by design.

Di Angelo motioned toward a nearby detective, deliberately avoiding using his name. His voice was demanding but calm. "Cut her zips." He rolled his eyes as if to say, "Come on, we all know this is bullshit protocol."

"Yes, sir," the detective replied, already reaching into the front pocket of his vest. He pulled out a pair of surgical-grade scissors and stepped forward, crouching beside Dawn with quiet efficiency.

He snipped the plastic, and the zips fell to the ground. Dawn rubbed her wrists, red with pressure marks, then pulled her children into her arms, holding them tighter than she ever had before. Making eye contact with Roberts, Di Angelo asked, "How are we making out, brotha?" He whispered softly, moving into the other room, making sure Roberts was following his lead.

Roberts said softly, "He's basically confessed, Cap. Says he only saw young girls on some porn sites, but didn't search for it. Silva has the laptop we found in the dude's briefcase and is dumping it now.

The older girl, whose name is Nina, is crying and definitely knows something. Son of a bitch did something with her for sure."

Di Angelo shook his head. "Contact Agent Jenna Bennette from Child Abuse, have her talk with the kids and mom. She's great with kids. Let the scumbag's wife know what's going on. See if she knows anything more than she's letting on.

The spouse or partner always gets some level of hindsight when the truth is finally exposed."

"Copy that, Cap," Roberts replied.

Di Angelo walked past Hanlon, sitting on a wooden chair near the kitchen table, shirtless, squirming in his white jockey briefs. Di Angelo purposely avoided making eye contact and refrained from questioning him, blending in as if he were just one of the team members, not the commander of the entire investigation. Other HTCU members continued their search, combing through the home for digital devices, computers, and anything that could contain illicit material.

Allen Hanlon started yelling, "Somebody is buying me a new front door. Mother fuckers!" He shouted as he stared at the splintered front door.

He tried peeking around the corner to see what was developing in the other room with his wife and kids. But he could only see the back of his wife's head.

A female detective in black BDUs was partially obstructing his view.

"A busted door? That's the least of your problems," Di Angelo muttered out of sight from Hanlon but well within earshot. His voice was low and flat. Then, raising it just enough for the others to hear, he added, "Make sure the team leader, looking over at McKeown with a satirical smirk, documents the damage to the door. Full report."

A quiet ripple of laughter came from the next room. Entry team members appreciated a sharp jab.

McKeown, the team leader, stood amidst the debris: wood splinters, brass hinges, and bolts strewn across the entranceway. His helmet and balaclava concealed everything but his eyes. The slight squint in them revealed a smirk beneath the fabric. He glanced at Di Angelo and, without a word, casually flipped him the finger, his assault rifle resting calmly across his chest, his face controlled and composed.

Di Angelo caught the gesture and gave a subtle wink in response. He understood exactly what McKeown meant, just as he knew how deliberately it had been delivered. But he didn't smile. Not here. Not now. There were victims nearby. This wasn't entertainment, not for him, and certainly not for the innocent people huddled on the sofa.

Around him, members of the HTCU task force moved with surgical precision, scouring the house for anything that might store illicit digital material, computers, hard drives, or even broken, outdated cell phones. No detail was too small. No corner too clean.

Di Angelo's gaze swept the room. Something drew his attention, a small end table in the far corner, topped with marble and fitted with a single drawer. Normally, furniture like that would be left open during a sweep, its contents cleared. But this drawer remained shut.

He stepped over, crouched, and pulled it open.

Inside sat a Bible. Well-worn. Slightly askew.

He flipped open the cover.

"To Dawn, Happy Confirmation! Love, Mom."

Turning the delicate pages, his finger paused at the Book of Matthew, Chapter 18, verse 6. He circled the verse silently with his finger, murmuring under his breath:

"Whoever causes one of these little ones who believe in me to sin…"

He reached into the front pocket of his vest and retrieved a yellow highlighter, uncapping it with his teeth in a practiced motion.

Suddenly, his walkie crackled, sharp and loud against the tense quiet.

"Hey, Cap, we found it," came Silva's voice.

"Received. I'm on my way," Di Angelo replied.

He clicked the cap back onto the highlighter, still holding it in his mouth, and set the Bible gently on the tabletop, left open.

As he moved toward the front of the house, now little more than a splintered hole in the wall, with jagged metal clinging to the doorframe, he passed Detective Natalie Morel, who was geared up and alert.

He raised the highlighter.

"Table down the hall," he said firmly.

She nodded in silence and took the highlighter from his outstretched hand. Her boots thudded softly on the hardwood as she headed toward the corner table. The Bible lay waiting, its pages slightly curled at the edges.

She paused, leaned over, and read the verse that had captured Di Angelo's attention.

Then, with deliberate care, she highlighted Matthew 18:6, the yellow ink casting a quiet glow over the ancient warning etched in scripture.

Once finished, she closed the Bible gently, as if sealing away something sacred, or damning. She carefully tucked it back inside the drawer and closed it. Outside, beside the hum of the mobile forensics lab, she tossed the highlighter back to Di Angelo without a word.

"All good?" the captain asked.

"Yes, sir."

Without hesitation, Di Angelo stepped into the mobile lab parked at the curb in front of the residence. The door shut behind him with a click.

"What've we got, guys?" he asked, his tone sharp, ready.

Detective Silva turned in her chair, disbelief tightening her features as she slowly shook her head. "This guy's unbelievable," she said, her voice edged with disgust. "Dom, this guy has videos of his kids and their friends getting undressed, sleeping, just weird stuff. Tons of child pornography. Looks like there's a hidden camera in their basement and some other rooms. There's even footage of what looks like a sleepover. A bunch of cell phone videos dumped onto his computer and saved in a file titled 'Nina pool party.'"

She continued, her words clipped. "He's videoing the pool party. When someone comes over to speak with Allen, or he calls them over pretending to take a picture of the girls, he's actually recording. He angles the cell camera to point at their chests, their groin area, and their feet. Major foot fetish, tons of bare feet pics, mostly of the older daughter."

"What a freak," Silva muttered under her breath. She kept cataloging and tagging files for evidence, her stomach already tight from what she'd seen. One folder caught her attention: it was titled Home Alone, with the movie's poster featuring a young Macaulay Culkin as the cover image. She double-clicked. Inside were several promotional stills from the actual movie, but nestled among them was something else. Still shots. Of Nina.

Silva froze. Her heart sank. "Is that the little girl? Is the older one in there? Oh God…" she whispered, bile rising in her throat. "He videoed his own kid touching him. Look, he's making her touch him with her bare feet. Damn it."

Silva placed her head down on her laptop keyboard and stayed there for a moment, trying to clear away what she had just seen. "Damn it. This guy should be hung by his, " She cut herself off, voice breaking.

It was barely 7 a.m., and already Silva had seen more than most people could stomach in a lifetime. This wasn't her first child pornography case, unfortunately, far from it. But this one cut deeper. The perpetrator wasn't some faceless predator on the dark web. It was the father of the little girl sitting barely twenty-five yards away.

She'd worked enough of these cases to know the imagery, the horror. There was always a measure of psychological distance when the files came stamped with foreign text, when it looked like they'd come from somewhere else: Russia, China, anywhere but here. That distance was gone now. This was local. This was personal. This was real and in her face. And that made it worse.

She skipped to the next video.

A child's giggle echoed faintly from another video Conners had playing on his forensic computer screen, but in Dominic's mind, it blurred into something older, familiar. A laugh from long ago.

His jaw clenched as the memory returned, uninvited.

He was back in the classroom at St. Magnus's, sitting near the back, where sunlight slanted through the high windows, making billions of dust particles visible as they floated lazily in the light. The room smelled of chalk, old wood polish, and something faintly sour, the kind of scent that clings to memory. Fifty years could pass, and that smell would still hit like a ghost. One breath, and you were back in that cramped classroom, clutching a Ticonderoga pencil in a sweaty fist.

Father Asher stood at the front of the room, arms spread wide in a slow, almost theatrical gesture.

"I'd like some of you to come forward," he said, "and let me wash your feet, just as Jesus did for his disciples."

A ripple of laughter stirred among the students, awkward, fidgety.

Dominic leaned toward his confidant, his secretly closest friend, Thomas Hawk. He'd always liked Thomas's name. Dominic had loved birds for as long as he could remember and wished *his* first name had been Hawk.

Hawk Di Angelo, he thought. *Yeah, that had a pretty good ring to it.*

He could almost hear Thomas's low, teasing whisper: "No way am I letting this guy touch my feet. That's some freaky shit, right?"

He could see Thomas's easy grin, the casual shrug that always preceded trouble.

"I'd let him wash mine if it got me outta summer school," Thomas would've said, flashing the lopsided smile he wore whenever he was scheming. "Shit, I'd wash *Asher's* feet if it meant I didn't have to be stuck in here all summer."

Dominic smirked, shaking his head. "No way. I'm not spending one extra second in this oven with Asher breathing down my neck. But I need extra credit or a miracle to pass his stupid class. Just thinking about Father Asher's nasty feet is enough to make me puke," Dominic said to himself. Then he glanced over at a girl sitting two rows from him, her head down. Her profile was hidden by her long hair. "I'd wash Jasmine Dallas' feet, though. One at a time!" He said softly to Thomas. Jasmine sat, twirling a strand of her light brown hair around her finger. His stomach did a stupid little flip. He didn't notice Father Asher gliding silently down the aisle until the priest's voice, sharp and cold, cracked across the room: "Get a good look, boy. Because while she's at the pool this summer, you'll be here, sweating over scripture. Eyes back in your head!" The entire class turned and faced Dominic. His chest tightened. His face flared hot with embarrassment. "Why the hell would he do that?" Dominic thought, his anger rising. He wouldn't look at Jasmine ever again. He stared down at the scratched desktop, feeling the weight of every kid's gaze pressing on him. Somewhere, he was sure of it, Thomas was hiding a laugh behind his hand, which made the whole thing hurt a little less. As Father Asher turned and walked away, a few kids dared to giggle, low, nervous sounds, the kind that fizzled out as fast as they started.

Captain Di Angelo blinked, the fog of memory clearing as the harsh fluorescent lights of the mobile lab reasserted themselves. The distant echo of a child's laughter, the kind that once came from trust and innocence, faded into the background hum of servers and the soft clicks of evidence bags being sealed.

He straightened, eyes scanning his team. His detectives were still reviewing footage and logging devices with grim focus. He placed a steady hand on Silva's shoulder.

"Alright," he said quietly, voice low but firm. "We've got more than enough to bury this guy. I want everything cataloged, every file cross-referenced. Not a single minute of this sick bastard's footage slips through the cracks."

Silva gave a sharp nod and began breaking down her equipment.

"Make sure that the hard drive from Hanlon's briefcase gets priority imaging," Di Angelo added, then turned toward Conners. "And loop in the Child Abuse Unit. I want preliminary charges filed before this scumbag even makes it to holding."

"Copy," Conners replied. His eyes lingered for a moment on the screen, where freeze-frames from the pool party video still glowed, children mid-laughter, frozen in time.

Di Angelo's thoughts spiraled.

Little girls laughing, acting like kids. Innocent. And this bastard, scoping them out for his sick gratification. Their father.

Homicide scenes were easier. Cleaner, in a way. The blood washed away. The dead didn't suffer anymore. But this? This stuck to the soul.

"Let's make sure Mrs. Hanlon knows exactly what we found here today," he said after a beat. "Especially that 'Home Alone' file Silva uncovered, and the cell phone videos he took of his kids and their friends at the pool. There are a lot of unaware victims here."

He looked around the lab, voice edged with quiet respect.

"Nice work, guys."

The words were genuine, though his tone carried the weight of defeat. Then he exhaled slowly, as if letting go of something he hadn't realized he'd been holding in.

Turning toward the exit, he stepped down the first metal stair, calling back over his shoulder, "I gotta head back to the office, talk with the chief."

His boots hit the pavement with a dull thud.

"We're charging this asshole with everything you can think of, especially manufacturing 'cp' *child porn.*"

"Wrap it up," he said. "I'm getting hungry. Could go for some warm, fluffy pancakes, coffee, and a side of bacon at Amy's Diner."

It was the ritual. After every morning raid, no matter how brutal, they always said it.

"Let's get breakfast."

It didn't fix anything. But it made things a little more bearable. A little less fucked up.

Comfort food for the troops.

Especially for Di Angelo. Breakfast had always been his favorite meal, pancakes ranking right up there with spaghetti and meatballs. But more than the food, it was the shift in atmosphere. The rhythm changed. The conversation lightened. It gave them all a few quiet minutes to scrape off the filth they'd just waded through.

It was the soap and water they needed to wash away the images that burned behind their eyes.

Even if only for a little while.

Chapter 3

Awall of floor-to-ceiling windows revealed the gritty sprawl of Camden City. Inside the bottleneck-shaped, 18-story building located at 5th and Market, the High-Tech Crimes Unit Task Force had occupied its space for the past two years.

On the sixth floor, the air buzzed with the mechanical rhythm of printers, the occasional ring of a desk phone, and the low murmur of voices discussing things better left unheard. Files stood stacked on desks like quiet monuments to heinous sex crimes. The place smelled of stale coffee and warm circuitry, bureaucracy and burnout mingling into a single, bitter scent.

"HTCU TASK FORCE" was printed in bold on the door leading in from the lobby. He pushed through it, a folder tucked under his arm. His gait was crisp, his expression unreadable.

The weight of the morning, what he'd seen, and more so what it had awakened in him, lingered. Memories of Father Asher, St. Magnus, and Jasmine Dallas drifted in like cold air from a cracked window. Uninvited, but impossible to ignore.

Di Angelo chuckled softly, a dry sound, just a puff of air through his nose. Some memories lifted his spirits, like when "A Horse with No Name" by America drifted from a radio speaker. It brought back flashes of sunlight, handlebars, the high dive at the public pool, and TV shows like *Gilligan's Island* and *The Six Million Dollar Man*.

Those memories had aged like fine wine, mellowing with time, growing more precious the older he got.

Others… aged like rotting crabs.

Father Asher. The stench of his cigarettes masked something fouler that clung to his clothes. The echo of his footsteps still haunted the corridors of St. Magnus. Those memories didn't mellow with time; they fermented. They clawed at Dominic, lodged deep in the folds of his brain, refusing to fade. That damn school hallway, the one that always smelled like floor wax and bagged lunches.

It all sat just beneath the surface, like a bruise that never quite healed.

But here, in this office, none of that had a place. The past didn't breathe here. This was all business. Here, he wasn't Dominic. He was Captain Di Angelo. And the weight of that crown wasn't just heavy, it was earned.

As Di Angelo headed toward his appointment with the chief, an attractive woman looked up from behind her monitor as he passed by her office, Assistant Prosecutor Lani Hale. Sharp-eyed, thirty-something, with a figure that turned heads and a wardrobe that didn't hide it.

***

"Hey, Cap," Lani called as she stood up from her desk.

The soft, slate-gray dress she wore hugged her curves like it had been tailored just for her, smooth and tight in all the right places. Di Angelo scanned her from head to toe in a split second, a talent unknowingly honed during his eight years of Catholic school. You never got caught staring at the plaid skirts. Not with the nuns roaming the halls like hawks circling their prey. Hawks in habits. One wrong glance and your day was shot. So you adapted, learned the art of the peripheral.

Vision sharpened by survival. Faster, smarter. Like the Six Million Dollar Man, his Monday night ritual back in the seventies. We have the technology…

Lani's blouse underneath was unbuttoned just enough to tease the young interns, the subtle dip revealing a glimpse of the soft line between her breasts. Her skin was smooth, golden, naturally tanned, and flawless, like shimmering silk. Her hair, straight and glossy, fell around her shoulders in waves of deep jet black. It reminded him of his wife's. He pushed the thought aside quickly, as if she were there watching him check out the talent.

Lani had once told Di Angelo she was Polynesian. He hadn't forgotten. How could he? She had a face like a hula dancer. All she was missing was a grass skirt and a flower in her hair.

Every male detective in the office noticed her when she passed. Not just because she was beautiful, but because she carried herself with a quiet composure that made you think twice before approaching with some dumb line just to get her attention. She was sharp, confident, the kind of woman who didn't need to demand attention to have it. Whether walking the halls of the sixth floor, striding through a courtroom, or crossing the parking garage with purpose in her heels, every head turned. Of course they did.

What Di Angelo admired most about her, though, wasn't any of that. It was her unflinching, genuine passion for working CP cases. Many attorneys tried to help with those kinds of investigations, but for one reason or another, it became too much to carry. Too much darkness to bring home. Or they simply didn't mesh with the detectives, couldn't make the cut. No one wanted to stare into hell every day. Di Angelo understood that. He never guilted anyone for leaving the unit.

When their eyes met, she caught the exhaustion behind Di Angelo's stare, the kind that settled into the bones after years of witnessing the unimaginable. She knew it well. It didn't just come from long hours or bureaucratic headaches; it came from the darkness they both hunted.

Still, beneath it, his tenacity remained. She respected that. Admired it. Attempted to match it. "Cap," she said, nodding toward the folder in his hand. "That's the case from this morning?"

Di Angelo slowed, letting her catch up. Without a word, he pivoted slightly, waiting for her to fall into step beside him. He gave a tight nod and handed it over.

"Allen Hanlon," Di Angelo began, his voice flat and clinical. "Wife is Dawn Hanlon. They've got two daughters, Danny, five, and Nina, seven. Nina is definitely a victim. We found hidden cameras in the basement, bedrooms… even the bathroom. He cataloged everything. Cellphone videos, too, birthday parties, pool parties, sleepovers. And one particularly nasty one. He and his seven-year-old daughter."

He paused just long enough for the weight of it to sink in. "Charges will include possession, distribution, and manufacturing. Move fast, Counselor, and you'll be able to tack on everything else you can think of. The seven-year-old indicated she was violated by her father. Child Abuse is scheduled to interview her later today at their satellite office."

Without waiting for a reply, Di Angelo turned into his office. The door was wide open. He moved behind his desk, peeled off his tactical vest, and dropped it beside the chair. The Velcro gave easily, worn down from too many hits, too many mornings just like this.

Lani lingered in the doorway, watching silently. She'd heard about how the captain conducted himself in the field. She'd heard he had rage in his voice when he confronted predators, heard about the precision in how he moved through raids. But now, as he removed his gear, she watched the armor fall away, literally and otherwise. It felt like watching Superman take off his cape, revealing the man underneath.

Without asking, she sat on the edge of his desk. The air between them thickened. Not romantic. Just respect, and something else harder to name. Shared sentiments of the victims, maybe. The weight of doing this kind of work and still showing up for it the next day.

"You okay?" she asked finally, her voice quieter than usual.

Di Angelo didn't answer right away. He dropped into his chair and rubbed the back of his neck. "No," he said. "But I will be."

With a heavy breath, she flipped open the folder. Her eyes scanned the top page, and then she stilled, jaw tightening as the details sank in. "He recorded his own kid," she asked quietly.

"The older one," Di Angelo said grimly. "Don't know yet if the five-year-old was involved in daddy's foot games. Obsessed with her feet. Her feet all over him."

Shaking his head, he said, "Sick dude filmed her friends. Her seven-year-old friends are sleeping and using the bathroom. It's... messed up. Brace yourself when you read Silva and Conners's reports. Really, brace yourself when you view the video!"

"You'll never unsee what he made his kid do with her feet. Her little feet. So be ready, Counselor. Fair warning. Knocked Silva for a loop."

Di Angelo could feel the rage boiling back up. Hot acid clawed at his throat, the way it always did when the job stopped being about evidence and started being about evil. He was getting pissed all over again, because it wasn't just a case file anymore. It was a little girl. Her little feet. Her innocence. And some depraved fuck had turned all of it into content for his pleasure. Maybe others, too.

For a moment, neither of them spoke. The room held its breath.

Di Angelo turned, almost absently, and said, "Alexa, resume music."

"Playing the station, Smooth Jazz," came the soft robotic reply.

The sultry tones of Dave Koz drifted into the office. Di Angelo eased back into his high-backed leather chair, the creak of the worn upholstery the only sound besides the saxophone's slow moan.

"I don't know how you do it, Cap. How your unit goes through this shit every day." Lani shook her head, a yellow legal pad in her hand. "I'll draft preliminary charges and get a judge on the line for a rush remand."

Di Angelo nodded but lingered a second longer. "Push for no bail," he said. "Guy's got some bullshit charges in his past. Looks like somebody's neighbor, though. The kind that slips through cracks. Plus, he's got a political hook."

Lani studied the name on the folder. "He's not related to James Hanlon, is he? Supreme Court Judge James Hanlon?! Please say no, Cap."

"Okay, no. But yes, he is."

"How the hell did you get around the judge with a search warrant? That judge is gonna lose his seat!"

Shaking her head, Lani laughed. The sound was soft, low. "Who else knows?" she asked.

"Like I give a shit," Di Angelo replied swiftly.

Still perched on the edge of his desk, Lani stood, her body hesitating for a moment, caught between impulse and professionalism. Part of her wanted to say something, reassure him that he could count on her.

Tell him it was going to be okay. That no matter what happened in court, she had his back.

But the thought passed. Professionalism demanded restraint. And restraint had its own quiet power.

Di Angelo stood too. "I gotta see the Chief, give him the update. Then meet the gang for breakfast. You should come sometime," he added.

Lani smiled, soft but teasing. "Thanks, Cap. But I think a prosecutor at a table full of cops might kill the vibe. It'd be like having breakfast with monks."

"Nah," he said, waving it off. "My guys? They've got nothing to hide." The sarcasm in his tone was light but not missed.

Their eyes met for a brief second, and both let out a quiet laugh.

As Lani turned to leave, Di Angelo reached out, resting his hand lightly against her back as they stepped out of his office. He appreciated her. Cases like these had a way of pulling the team closer, like soldiers huddled in a foxhole, waiting for the enemy to breach the wall.

They'd been working together for a solid two years, their chemistry a constant source of amusement in the unit. A steady stream of ball-busting, inside jokes, and low-key bickering had led plenty of people to assume something was going on between them.

There wasn't. And he didn't care what others thought.

Anyone who truly knew Di Angelo understood one thing: he had one woman in his life, and her name was Ann. If anyone ever questioned it, all they had to do was look at the ink on his left arm: her name, bold and permanent, like his love for her.

Lani was simply the best assistant prosecutor for the unit. Over the past two years, she'd worked hard to understand the technology, even joining them on predator stings to see firsthand what it was really like. It was rare for an assistant prosecutor to want to know what went on in the streets, to be part of the action, not just armchair it from behind a desk and read the results with their morning coffee.

He fumbled for his keys, told Lani to keep him updated with the charges, then headed down the hall to speak with the Chief before grabbing breakfast with his team.

***

The authentic, old-school doorbell gave a tired jingle as Di Angelo stepped into Amy's Diner. It was the kind of place that hadn't changed in decades. Laminated menus were stuck to the edges of the table. Vinyl booths were patched at the corners with matching strips of colored duct tape. A jukebox that hadn't worked right since the Reagan administration.

Barb, the waitress, had been working here since before half the cops in Camden were born.

Silva and Conners were already at their usual booth, hunched over one side, laughing about something on Silva's phone. Silva looked up as Di Angelo slid into the seat across from them.

"Catch any more bad guys on the way over, Dom?" she asked, raising her coffee mug.

"What took you so long?" Conners added with a grin, glancing at Silva, a smirk tugging at the corner of his mouth. "Cap? How come she gets to call you 'Dom'?"

Di Angelo didn't break stride. He turned just enough to catch Silva in his periphery, deadpan, then reached for the glass of water already waiting for him. He sipped it, picked up the plastic menu, and

43

pretended to read it.

He already knew what he wanted. They all did.

"Believe me, I've tried, Sarge. No respect. Just won't give me the respect of the rank I deserve." He paused, then added, "But as long as she keeps pulling kiddie porn off the phones and hard drives of these sick, twisted bastards, she can call me whatever the hell she wants."

Connie Silva and Di Angelo had a unique relationship.

She was sharp, attractive, and a total ballbuster. They'd first clicked back when she was just working IT, before the badge, before the gun. Before, she was identified only as "Silva." Di Angelo had seen something in her back then, something wasted on setting up workstations and resetting passwords across the county. He'd convinced her to join the force, knowing she was made for more.

The academy had been no problem; she was fit, focused, and tougher than most of the guys already on the job. Though they constantly broke each other's stones, Di Angelo never steered her wrong. He cared about her career, her safety, and the kind of detective she'd become. Over time, he became her mentor, her confidant, and her closest friend on the job. They knew each other's weaknesses and covered each other's blind spots. In the field, that kind of trust was everything.

During search warrants, Di Angelo always watched her back more than the others. He'd been the one to convince her to choose a career in law enforcement, and the thought of her getting hurt by a freak accident or a madman with a gun was something he couldn't stomach. If she approached a door carelessly or cut corners on safety, Di Angelo would call her out, but only after the job was done, and only when they were alone. In the car. In his office. That was the only time she gave him her full respect.

The team knew she was his favorite, and neither one ever denied it.

Silva grinned and shrugged, locking eyes with Conners. "Knew him back before he was 'big shit.' Besides, I call him 'Captain' when the brass is around. Got to keep up appearances."

Conners laughed. "And what am I?"

Silva tilted her head, mock-thinking. Then the smirk hit. "Brass... minus the 'BR.' But you know I love ya, Conners. I mean, Sergeant Conners."

Di Angelo shook his head, amused. A faint smirk touched his face as he raised a hand to Barb, signaling for his usual, pancakes and bacon on the same plate.

Barb waved and shouted, "Hey, Dom! Coming up, Sweetie."

He leaned back in the booth and let out a breath, his shoulders finally starting to ease.

"Just trying to forget what I can't unsee," he muttered.

There was a beat of silence.

"You wanna talk about it?" Silva asked, her voice more serious than usual.

The team all knew the job was physical, sure, but muscle strains and broken bones healed a hell of a lot easier than a broken mind. This kind of shit? It was cancerous. Ate away at your brain, your psyche, and your longevity on the job.

Di Angelo shook his head. "Nah. I'm good." He managed a faint smile. "Tonight, I'll pour a bourbon and catch up on my bird logs. I'm a week behind."

Di Angelo's pastime: birds and bourbon, his favorite way to crush the weight of the day.

It was simple, but it scratched the same itch that made him a good cop. Any bird that landed in his yard or stopped by his feeders got logged in a notebook or snapped with his phone. Like the names and faces of defendants, bird calls and species came to him naturally, etched into memory without effort. It gave him something to study that didn't hurt anyone. Something pure.

Birds didn't lie. Didn't hurt anyone. They just came and went. Filled their bellies with sweet nectar or sunflower seeds under a watchful eye.

His nectar was a neat bourbon.

Silva smiled and shook her head. "You and those birds. I get the bourbon, Dom, but birdwatching? You're getting old, dude."

She reached across the table and gently poked a finger toward his chest, just barely making contact, as if testing to see if he was real or still reachable.

"And you're getting daring with that finger, girl," Di Angelo shot back. "You'd better hope you're in my shape when you're my age."

Silva made a hissing noise through her teeth. "What, 80? Eat your pancakes, old head. Or do you need me to feed you?"

"Ha," Dom snorted, shaking his head. "No respect. You'll miss me when I'm gone."

"You better not leave us!" Silva fired back. She knew Di Angelo was closing in on his time with the county and had begged him to become chief.

"Yeah, okay. Shut up and eat your yogurt parfait."

They all laughed quietly as Barb brought three more placemats over to the table.

"I assume the others are coming?"

"Yes, ma'am," Conners answered.

Outside, the neon sign above Amy's Diner buzzed and stuttered, casting a sickly pink light over the cracked pavement steps. Three more detectives, still in their gear, stinking of sweat and stale adrenaline, pushed through the door and joined the others without a word. They looked like hell, faces hollowed by sleepless nights and the shit they couldn't unsee from the morning hit.

McKeown slid in next to Silva. She didn't mind.

Nicolella added a chair to the end of the table. "I'm starving," he said.

Hearing that made Di Angelo feel good. That meant Nicolella had left the job and all the images on his forensic computer behind. Not in his head.

The plates of food in front of them helped. Grease, salt, and heat had a way of grounding you, if only for a while. For a few moments, the chewing dulled the noise in their heads. Jokes got passed around like napkins. A weak laugh here. A crooked smile there.

The kind of insults that, if you didn't understand the bond between these kinds of cops, would sound brutal, devastating, even. But in here, it meant respect. Brotherhood. Survival.

But the medicine that breakfast at Amy's Diner provided only lasted while sitting in the booth. They all knew that.

The relief was temporary, like cheap liquor or borrowed time. Because sometimes, the worst memories weren't the ones caught on tape. They were the ones that wormed their way into your gut and stayed there. The ones you had to carry alone, long after the case was closed and the world moved on.

After breakfast, Di Angelo drove in silence, the low hum of tires on asphalt giving rhythm to the thoughts grinding in his head. The city blurred past his windows, row homes leaning tiredly against each other, chain-link fences tangled with dead vines. He wasn't really seeing any of it.

His mind ran in a dozen directions, like it had for years, bringing on migraines, insomnia, and chronic aches: heartburn, a stiff neck, and a back that never stopped throbbing.

A flashback came uninvited as he drove past St. Magnus School on his way back to the office. Camden Avenue was a shortcut to Route 130, and as he rolled past the rectory, the memory hit like a cold slap.

He remembered the day he sat outside that very building, waiting for Thomas. They were supposed to meet with Father Asher in his office. Not wanting to be late, Dominic had knocked firmly on the rectory door.

No answer.

He'd hesitated, then gave it a few more raps before slowly turning the knob. The door creaked open, and he leaned in just far enough to catch a glimpse of half the foyer and part of the hallway leading to Father Asher's office. A shadow of his head fell across the polished floor.

"Hello? Is there anyone here? Father Asher?" Dominic had called out softly.

Silence.

He stepped inside, his shoes making faint scuffs on the tile as the heavy door eased shut behind him. The rectory air was cold, carrying a trace of pine and the musty scent of old carpet, odor sealed in too long behind unopened windows.

He crept down the dim hallway, ears attuned to every creak and whisper.

Then, voices.

One high-pitched, trembling. Maybe crying. Or laughing? The tone wavered in that strange space between fear and forced joy.

Then came the unmistakable voice of Father Asher, calm, measured, and disturbingly warm.

"There, that's how trust is built. That's why you will succeed in this school."

Dominic stopped cold. He was just outside the office door now, careful not to breathe too loudly, heart pounding in his chest. He quickly tiptoed back to the foyer and lowered himself onto a small bench resting against the wall outside the rectory assistant's office. His heart thudded, breath shallow, as if the walls themselves might whisper what he'd just overheard.

Then, footsteps.

Dominic could hear the door to Asher's office open. Two sets of steps headed down the hall in his direction.

"Hi, Father," Dominic said with a short wave as they approached.

"Oh. Hello, boy," Asher replied, unrolling his sleeve.

The two boys made eye contact. They had met once in the schoolyard. The kid was new to St. Magnus. A sixth grader. He had an accent.

That's why Dominic remembered him.

"Hey," Dominic said as the boy walked past him.

"Hey," the boy whispered back.

The priest held the door for the kid with the accent and told him, "Come back next week." As the door closed, Asher turned to Dominic and said, "Follow me, boy."

They entered Asher's office. The room was small and cold, smelling faintly of incense and mildew. A crooked crucifix hung on the wall. Papers cluttered the desk in front of Father Asher, half-graded assignments, lesson plans, and something more insidious layered beneath it all.

Dominic sat stiffly across from him, fingers twitching nervously, tapping a silent, erratic tune on his thigh like a pianist unsure of the next note.

Eighth grade had never felt so old.

"You know..." Father Asher's voice was soft, almost coaxing, "There's still a way to avoid summer school."

Just as he said that, a soft knock interrupted them. It was Thomas.

Dominic was thankful to see him.

Thomas had clearly heard what Asher said about there being a way to avoid summer school. "I'll do anything, Father," he blurted out as he sat next to Dominic.

Asher didn't comment on his lateness or the desperation in his voice. His focus remained fixed on Dominic.

He leaned back, folding his fingers like he was settling in for confession.

"You didn't volunteer for the foot washing," Asher said. "Why should I believe you really care about passing my class? Do you think you're better than Christ? Better than the apostles?"

The boys squirmed in their seats.

"Nobody really wanted to do it, Father. It's... kind of embarrassing," Thomas mumbled, eyes down.

A slow smile crept across Asher's face.

"Embarrassment," he said, "is a sign the soul is no longer innocent... and your brain is unintelligent."

The words landed like stones. Dominic blinked, unsure whether he was being insulted or guided.

Asher let the silence linger. Then, gently:

"If you let me practice with you now, just the ritual of foot washing, nothing more, the extra credit could make the difference. Enough for me to pass you. A gesture of trust... between us."

He made a small, circling motion with his hand to include the three of them.

They didn't answer, not right away. They just stared at the desk, then at each other, caught under the weight of expectation.

Dominic felt a tightness in his gut. The walls felt closer. The crucifix looked more crooked. Still, after a moment, he gave a small nod.

Thomas went along, not with a nod, but with a tilt of the head and a raised shoulder. If Dominic was okay with it, then so was he.

Father Asher stood and walked toward the small bathroom inside his office. The only way in or out was through that room.

It was even colder than the office, tiled in pale green, the kind that always looked sick under fluorescent light. A rusted pipe hissed behind the wall. The mirror over the sink was streaked with age and disuse.

Thomas entered first.

***

Father Asher closed the door behind him and told Dominic to wait.

The bathroom wasn't large enough for all three, so he carried a chair inside with him.

Thomas sat on the edge of a metal chair, shoes neatly placed to the side, socks tucked inside them. His bare feet rested in a plastic basin as Asher filled it with tepid tap water. The skin on his heels was pink, flushed more from embarrassment than temperature.

Father Asher knelt in front of him, sleeves rolled up, hands steady. He poured the water slowly over Thomas's feet, the sound unnervingly gentle, like rain on a rooftops. His voice dropped to a whisper, private, coaxing.

"I see how all the boys look at Jasmine Dallas… Beautiful girl," he said, lifting his eyes with a sly smile. "Did you know I heard her confession today?"

Thomas blinked, startled. His face wavered between curiosity and confusion.

"Dominic is always staring at her," Asher added, looking back down at Thomas's feet.

Thomas let out a nervous little laugh. "Yeah, he likes her a lot."

"She's full of secrets," Asher continued, his tone like a man unwrapping something delicate. "And I know them all. But she trusts me. As a priest, I've been given the gift to forgive. All your sins, washed away once confessed to me."

He smiled again. Crooked teeth, stained yellow from coffee and cigarettes.

The room seemed to shrink.

"Do you want to be forgiven for all your bad thoughts and actions?" he asked, voice sweet with menace. "Then you must trust me with your secrets, too."

The water kept pouring. The air grew thick.

The stench of Father Asher's breath, coffee, cigarettes, and something sour underneath, mixed with the reek of stale cologne. It formed a fog in the small room, coiling in Thomas's throat. He tried breathing through his mouth, but it didn't help. Every exhale from the priest hit him like a wave of rot and cheap aftershave.

His stomach turned.

Something inside him screamed to get up, to leave. But his legs stayed still, bare and damp, shifting around in that plastic basin like they didn't belong to him.

"To truly trust someone," Asher murmured, "is to create a sacred bond. Only the two of us and the Lord will understand. Prove to me you're worthy of that bond, that you're intelligent enough to carry it... and I will share secrets. And more. Your summer will be yours to enjoy."

The young boy, confused and desperate to get past the moment, stared down into the basin. The water reflected a shaky version of himself. His fingers clenched the edge of the chair.

He didn't speak.

Then, with quiet ceremony, Father Asher leaned in and pressed his lips to the top of the boy's foot.

Thomas closed his eyes tightly. Confused. Still clinging to everything he'd been taught; priests were the closest to God.

"Even if Father Asher didn't look the part, he had to be closer to God than me or Dominic was. He had to be. He was a priest," Thomas kept telling himself, convincing himself.

As the priest continued fondling Thomas's feet, something inside him snapped. He couldn't take it anymore.

In one swift motion, Thomas yanked his legs from the water, his wet foot smacking Asher across the face. The priest lunged, grabbing for him, but Thomas slipped free. He bent down fast, snatching up his shoes and socks in one hand, the other scrambling for the doorknob.

Seconds later, the bathroom door rattled as the frightened boy fumbled with it, hands shaking, breath shallow. He shoved it open, and it slammed against the plaster wall with a loud crack.

He bolted past Dominic like someone, or something, was chasing him.

"Thomas!" Dominic called out. "Wait up!"

Dominic ran as fast as he could. Thomas dipped into the schoolyard, squeezing through the rusted metal gates. He finally stopped beneath the metal cross and leaned against the beige bricks of the school wall. He threw his shoes to the ground, sat down, pulled on his socks, then slipped into his shoes and laced them up quickly.

As he stood, he felt winded. His shoulders were tight, his whole body stiff with shame.

When he finally faced Dominic, his cheeks were wet and blotchy, his eyes bloodshot and darting away.

"What happened? Is he gonna pass you?" Dominic asked, trying to keep his voice light, like it was any other day.

"Yeah, yeah, I'm good," Thomas mumbled. He wiped his face roughly with both hands. Then he stood in silence, shaking his head like he'd either committed a crime or just watched his favorite football team get shut out by a much lesser opponent.

Then, from complete silence, he blurted out, "I let him kiss my feet, Dom! I let Asher touch my bare feet! He was rubbing my feet and, and then he…"

Thomas leaned back against the beige brick. He looked up at the metal cross directly above his head. His fists clenched and unclenched like he wanted to punch the wall, or crawl out of his own skin.

Dominic studied him. Paced around him like a shadow.

He could feel Thomas's anxiety; something had gone wrong. Really wrong. But he didn't press too hard. Instead, he placed a hand on Thomas's back and patted it softly.

Thomas turned and looked directly at Dominic, like he was staring into a mirror. His eyes locked onto his friend's.

"Don't tell anyone we went to see that priest, Dom! That we went to Asher's office, or what happened to me in there. Promise me!" Thomas's voice flared with anger. He was rambling now. Dominic hadn't seen this intensity since their schoolyard fights, or when Thomas was sprinting to intercept a long bomb in two-hand touch.

"Okay, okay," Dominic said in a sad, low tone. "I promise."

A knot tightened in his stomach, heavy and cold.

He knew what had happened in the rectory bathroom was wrong. And he knew one thing for sure: he'd never step foot in Father Asher's office again.

He wanted to tell someone.

But he'd made a promise. The only thing he could do now was pray that he'd made the right choice.

Chapter 4

After surveilling a new brick-and-mortar target, this time a rowhome on the north side of Camden, Di Angelo couldn't help but feel that familiar tug in his gut. He'd spent years undercover in that city, buying heroin, making gun deals with Bloods and other unscrupulous thugs.

When Di Angelo spoke of his days in narcotics, he referred to them as the "good old days", when you knew exactly who the targets were, where they lived. What they stood for. No masks, no pretense. They were drug dealers and gun runners, living in one of the most dangerous cities in America. Tattoos marked their necks, foreheads, and fingers. Red bandanas around their heads or hanging from telephone poles marked their turf and allegiance. They never tried to hide who they were. In fact, hiding their colors or tattoos could get them killed by their own gang.

It was just the opposite of what investigations were like in other units, especially child porn jobs.

Back then, it was easy until it wasn't. Until someone from the inside got word to the targeted dealer that Di Angelo, aka Anthony Marzo, was possibly a cop. Then *you* became the target. And once they had confirmation you weren't who you said you were, they tried to kill you.

Other than that, life undercover, buying and selling dope or making gun deals at 3 a.m. on streets where, if you were white, you were either a cop, a lawyer, or an addict, Di Angelo had found his niche. Strange as it sounds, he'd felt comfortable there.

But even in Camden, the cancer of child porn addiction thrived. Unlike drugs and guns, it was hidden, tucked behind screens, masked by anonymity. It revealed itself only through an IP address pinging a server a few miles away. Most users had no idea what an IP address even was, let alone how that virtual trail of breadcrumbs could lead detectives straight to their front door.

Di Angelo pulled into his usual spot outside the PD, the tires crunching over loose gravel as he killed the engine. The hum of the car faded, but the noise in his head kept roaring: memories, questions, guilt, suspicion, all of it crowding his brain.

For a week now, memories of Thomas had drifted in and out of his mind, haunting him by day and tormenting him at night. That day. That kid. The memory he thought he'd buried long ago had clawed its way back to the surface, uninvited, unrelenting, and sharp as broken glass.

He stepped out, shutting the door harder than he meant to. The late afternoon heat hit him like a wet slap, but he didn't slow down. His boots struck the pavement with purpose.

A quick nod to the uniformed guard at the front post, "Hey, buddy," and a half-hearted wave.

No time for small talk. Not today.

Inside, the building hummed with its usual static: the faint whine of overworked printers, muffled conversations behind glass doors, the distant clack of heels echoing off linoleum. Normal. Professional. Cold.

Di Angelo wanted the noise to drown it out, the image of a boy fumbling at that doorknob, panic in his eyes, shame in his voice. The door slamming. The kid is running from something. A tough kid who stood up to anyone. Who actually *enjoyed* it when a bully picked on him, or on some weaker kid? That gave Thomas an excuse to throw fists and try out his boxing skills. However, he fought more like a hockey player than a boxer, reckless, headlong, punishing.

Di Angelo shook his head, trying to dislodge the memories. "Let it go," he muttered to himself as he stepped into the elevator.

But it was already too late for that.

His day was set to be filled with waiting, for fallout, for punishment, for another reminder that he'd recently locked up a Supreme Court judge's brother and acted like he had no idea who it was. He took the heat. And when the prosecutor grilled him for going rogue, he shrugged and said, "Just doing my job."

Because he *was*.

"I followed every protocol to the letter. Ask the judge who signed off," had been his defense the day they came at him.

He dodged the suits for a few days after that, but his patience was thinning.

Screw it. They can't fire me, he told himself.

But they could sure as hell sideline him, tuck him away in some dead-end unit like Grand Jury or Trial Team. No action. No lockups. Just paperwork and burnout. Surrounded by detectives who'd lost the fire. The ones punching a clock, counting the days to retirement. Guys who wouldn't know how to investigate their way out of a paper bag, and didn't care to try.

It was close to quitting time when Commissioner Mary Scola swept into the unit like a gust of sharp wind, eyes already scanning for her target.

"Di Angelo!" she called, her voice cutting clean through the din.

The captain stood near his desk, vest slung over the back of his chair. His stance had a lean to one side, back and knees worn down from too many years of disregard.

She spotted him and smiled widely.

"Nice job the other day," she said, striding over. "What does that make, thirty lockups so far this year? And it's only May!"

Di Angelo gave her a faint smile, but it didn't reach his eyes.

"Yeah," he said, voice low and rough. "We'll hit about twenty-five, thirty more before the year's over, I'm sure."

Scola caught the tone. Her grin faded, replaced by something more grounded. "What's the matter?" she asked, her voice quieter now. "If this job is getting to you or your guys, we'll switch it up. Cut back on the hits. You're running a warrant a week."

She shook her head.

"I love putting these sick bastards behind bars as much as you do, Dom. But don't burn out on me."

There was no bullshit between them. Never had been. That's the main reason she adored Di Angelo, no bullshit.

"You know who I locked up?" Di Angelo asked, his tone matter-of-fact.

"Indeed, I do! Don't worry." She was already shaking her head. "I cut the chief and the prosecutor off at the pass. Oh, they were pissed, already getting ready to transfer you to some bullshit unit. I told them you informed me before the hit and that I gave the green light." She leaned against the edge of his desk. "Listen, the fallout's going to be heavy around here for a while, but it'll pass."

Without a word, Di Angelo opened the bottom drawer of his desk and slid it wide. Nestled between paperwork and a spare holster sat a bottle of Jack Daniel's. He pulled it free along with two small glasses. Holding the bottle up with a half-smirk, he asked, "Want a swig?"

Scola didn't hesitate. "Yes."

He poured, handing her a glass. The dark amber liquid caught the light like a flame.

"This gonna get me fired, boss?" he asked.

Scola laughed under her breath, swirling the whiskey in her glass. "Would you like to be made chief? He's leaving in six months."

His smile faltered. He turned toward the window, eyes catching the hazy Philadelphia skyline, now fading into dusk. The weight in his shoulders returned.

"No thanks," he said flatly. "Being a captain's already political enough for me. I'm sick of watching my team bust their asses arresting these freaks, only for some weak-ass prosecutor to cut them a deal. Slap on the wrist, out in six months if they shed a tear in front of the judge."

He downed the drink in one swallow. The burn barely registered. He poured another for himself.

"And don't even get me started on the Fumbling Bumbling Idiots that fuck up every case they steal from me. They don't give a shit unless it boosts their stats. Hanlon, he's already got a plea deal in the works. Fucking unbelievable. Anyone else would be looking at twenty years minimum."

Scola winced but nodded. She knew it was true.

"So, you heard," Mary said quietly.

"He's not even in jail. They sent him home." Di Angelo's voice rose with disbelief. "He molested his own kid, Mare! And they sent him home! What the hell are we doing all this work for?"

His words dropped to a mumble, but Mary understood every syllable. She stood there silently, glass in hand.

"I wish I had an answer for you, Dom." She sat down slowly in one of the chairs opposite his desk.

"If you made me chief," Di Angelo went on, "you'd pull me off the streets. For good. And I can't do that."

"You shouldn't be on the streets. You're a *Captain*," she said, shaking her head, her voice rising just enough to register frustration, yet still low enough not to be heard outside his office door.

"I fight your chief every damn week about it. I don't know what you'll do without me when I'm gone." She took a small sip.

Di Angelo turned to her again, his face carved from stone, expressionless, unreadable.

"Keep fighting for me while you're still here, boss. These monsters are worse than drug dealers or murderers. I've dealt with both. They have *somewhat* of a conscience. These assholes kill something you can't get back: the innocence of a soul. Little innocent kids. Babies who have no idea what the world is about yet. No defense mechanisms to kick in."

His voice softened.

"Angels on earth, violated by devils wearing the faces of doctors, rabbis, teachers, coaches, priests, parents, the very people we're taught to trust when we're most vulnerable."

He looked Scola in the eyes.

"They don't deserve trials. They deserve bullets."

Mary lifted her glass once again.

"Keep swinging, Dom. Keep fighting your fight against these atrocious human beings. We'll win in the end because we battled them. We put the light on them. And now their families, friends, neighbors, damn, the whole world, know about their little dirty secrets once their name crosses your path. But next time, do me a favor and give me a heads-up if you lock up someone like Hanlon again."

She shook her head slightly and smiled.

He touched her glass with his.

"Salute, Mare."

"Salute," she echoed, and together they tossed back the Tennessee whiskey.

Mary set her glass on his desk and stepped forward, wrapping her arms around him.

It wasn't casual, it was grounding. The kind of hug that reminded him of Aunt Gia, the only woman who ever made him feel like someone was always in his corner, no matter how bad things got.

He wished he remembered the comfort of a hug from his mother.

The tight squeeze.

The long, steady pressure around his ribs.

The kind of hug only a mother can give to her son, a hug that says, *You're safe. Nothing can hurt you now.*

But he couldn't.

He could picture it in his mind; he'd even seen photos of them hugging, arms wrapped tight like they belonged nowhere else. But he couldn't remember the *feel* of it.

The warmth.

The protection.

Even now, at his age, he longed for a mother's hug.

Mary was several years older than Di Angelo. She was seasoned and carried herself like someone who had seen it all. Di Angelo respected the hell out of her.

"I mean it," she said, holding his gaze. "Keep doing you, Dom. I'm proud of you."

The words hit him hard, like a battering ram. His throat tightened.

His father used to say that, too, no matter the screw-up:

You tried. That's what matters. I'm proud of you.

It didn't matter what the outcome was: burning dinner, losing a football game, passing a test with a C-minus.

You tried. That's what matters. I'm proud of you, his father would say.

It was simple, unwavering, and for a kid like him, it meant everything.

Hearing it now, cracked something open inside.

He had a key person on his side. The rest could go to hell.

He tried not to think about Hanlon. Or the judge who cut him loose.

Just for a moment, he let it go.

The room fell silent.

Di Angelo found himself standing in the middle of his office, angry and confused. He wondered why God let things like this happen to children. Why He created people like that? Wondering if God made a mistake or had turned His back on humanity.

Or if He'd ever been watching to begin with.

Chapter 5

At a neglected diner called *The 541*, tucked off Route 9, the kind of place where the coffee came thick and burnt and no one paid attention to the conversations around them, Judy Malmuth stepped through the door, scanning for the man she was supposed to meet: Thomas Hawk.

Thomas had texted her where he'd be, third booth behind the checkout counter, against the wall. She spotted him as she turned right: baseball cap, salt-and-pepper stubble on his chin, sideburns peeking beneath the cap, and a nose that looked like it had met a fist or two. He wore black-framed tinted glasses and had the look of someone who'd seen too much and expected worse.

His large hand wrapped around a white mug, his finger too big for the handle to fit comfortably. He was sipping burnt coffee like it was medicine.

Judy approached cautiously, nerves tightening in her chest.

"Hawk?" she asked, her voice barely above a whisper.

He nodded. "Yes. Judy?"

Thomas was momentarily taken aback by how stunning Judy looked; it was unexpected. She wore black, skin-tight spandex that hugged her curves like a second skin. A cropped athletic jacket barely concealed the fitted tee underneath, its neckline just low enough to hint at what was beneath. Her frosted blonde hair was pulled back into a sleek ponytail. Her makeup was flawless, her lips glossed and inviting. Even her freshly manicured, deep red nails caught his eye.

She didn't just look good, she looked dangerous. Seductive. The kind of woman who knew exactly the effect she had on men. She didn't fit the scene. More like someone needing help fixing a flat. Not your average customer at *The 541,* for sure.

She gave a quick smile and slid into the booth, glancing around for any familiar faces.

"You can call me Thomas. Don't worry," he said, with a hint of a smile that never quite reached his mouth. "This isn't your kind of crowd. Relax. Nobody will recognize you in here."

Before Judy could fully settle into the booth, Thomas cut in, his voice firm, deep, and carrying what might have been a New York accent or just that "mob" sound, like a character from *The Godfather* or *The Sopranos.*

"Who gave you my number?"

She blinked, caught off guard.

"My friend Jackie. She got it from some guy she met at the gym. Used to be a cop or a fed, got hurt on the job, now works at Life Gym and Spa. Total musclehead."

He nodded slowly, the pieces already falling into place.

Judy continued. "Jackie was having trouble with this guy she went out with a couple of times. Started creeping her out, stalking her, showing up places. Threatened to kill her. Then she found out he was married. Total mess. She got scared and wanted to dig into the guy a little more.

The musclehead told her to call you. Said you were the one to talk to. Said you helped him out. Said you fix problems others can't touch."

Hawk let out a quiet, knowing breath. "Damon."

"She never called you, huh?" Judy asked.

"No," he said, with a small grin. "She didn't. Doesn't sound like the kind of case I would've taken on anyway."

"Well, lucky for her, the guy's wife pressed charges. Broke her jaw or something like that, when she accused him of cheating."

"He's in jail now, up in North Jersey somewhere. Domestic violence, assault, and some other stuff he had hanging over him."

Thomas leaned back slightly, eyes sharpening. "So how can I help you, Miss Judy?"

"This isn't easy to say," she began. "I believe… I think my husband is cheating on me. I don't know what to do. I don't want to call the police, because if I'm wrong, it could ruin his career. His life. Our lives."

Hawk stared at her, unreadable. He gave a faint smirk and straightened up, fiddling with the teaspoon beside his cup.

"Police don't usually get involved in cheating spouses, Judy," he said, his voice dry, with a hint of smugness.

"They do if the person he's cheating with is a girl," she snapped, jaw tight. "A young girl. Underage."

The words slipped through her lips like venom.

"What kind of evidence you got?" Thomas asked quietly.

"A couple of weeks ago, I overheard Marvin, my husband, on one of those Zoom calls," Judy said, her voice tight. "He's always in meetings, always on that damn laptop. Carries it everywhere. And God forbid I ever ask what he's doing or who he's talking to."

She glanced down, twisting the napkin in her lap.

"After this particular call, he got up from his desk and left the room. His laptop was still open, so I glanced at the screen, and I saw something. Something awful."

She looked up at Hawk, her face pale.

"There was another guy talking, but I couldn't see his face; it was blurred out. And Marvin's face… it looked like a robot. You know those Zoom filters that change your background or your face? That's what they were using."

She exhaled sharply, her fingers trembling.

"Marvin's mic was muted, but the other guy kept talking. Said he had what Marvin was looking for."

Next thing you know, there were eight, maybe ten girls. Little girls! They were sharing pics of naked little girls.

"Then I heard the hall bathroom door open and I panicked," Judy said, her voice dropping.

"I opened his desk drawer like I was looking for something, pen, paper, whatever, then slammed it shut and walked off, muttering to myself, 'Where the hell did I put that thing…' Just enough noise to make it look normal, not snoopy."

A waitress shuffled over to their table, her voice rough and gravelly, like someone who'd been chain-smoking since eighth grade.

The brass nameplate pinned to her chest read Erna, tilted slightly sideways like it couldn't be bothered to sit straight.

"You two ready to order?"

"Just another coffee," replied Thomas without looking up.

"And for you, honey?"

"Club soda with a lime slice, please," Judy said softly.

The waitress raised her notepad, pen already in hand. "That's it?"

"Yes, for now. Thanks," Judy replied.

"We only got lemon."

Judy nodded with a small, uneasy smile, barely meeting the waitress's eyes. "That's fine."

Judy took a breath and kept going.

"A few days later, at yoga, our friend Caitlin mentioned she saw Marvin at Cooper River Park. Said he was sitting at a picnic table with his niece, eating pizza from the Grill House over there."

Judy paused, watching Thomas's face for a reaction, then continued.

"I must've looked confused, because Caitlin kind of tilted her head and said, 'She was an adorable kid. Blonde hair, beautiful blue eyes.' She said she tried to say hi to the girl, but the girl didn't answer. Just looked down. Caitlin said she seemed really shy."

Judy's fingers tightened around her glass.

"I asked how old she looked. She said… 'Maybe twelve or thirteen?'"

Her eyes dropped to the table.

The waitress came by and placed the club soda in front of Judy, condensation dripping down the glass.

"Let me know when you're ready to order, guys," she muttered as she walked off, not waiting for a reply.

Thomas interjected briefly, "Is it uncommon for Marvin to take his niece out for lunch? To a park?"

Judy stared into his eyes. With short, breathy laughs through her nose, she said, "Marvin doesn't have a niece. Neither do I."

A long pause settled between them. Then Judy said, "My husband's got friends in high places. Real power. Feds. Judges. He knows how to cover things up. He brags about it."

Her eyes filled as she looked down at the table.

"I need to get away from him," she whispered. "I wish he would just… die."

The words hung there, suspended like a noose.

Thomas stirred his coffee, watching the swirl of cream settle.

"What's your husband do for a living?"

Judy answered without hesitation, her tone almost automatic, like she'd said it a hundred times before.

"He deals in federal government bids. Medical devices, mostly overseas. Multi-million-dollar contracts that always seem to just… fall into his lap."

Thomas raised an eyebrow. "Sounds lucrative."

"It is," she replied, her voice flat. "He travels a lot, Japan, Tokyo, the Netherlands. Gone for weeks at a time."

"Do you ever go with him?"

She shook her head once, firm. "Nope. Company policy. No spouses allowed on business trips."

He didn't respond. Just took a slow sip from his mug, letting the silence settle.

"Can you help?" Judy's voice was barely above a whisper, her eyes glassy, fighting off tears.

Thomas stayed calm, steady.

"You haven't called the cops because you're afraid his connections will bury it. And now you want me to believe you just stumbled into all this in the last couple of weeks? You've been married how long?"

"Five years," she said quietly.

Thomas pressed his lips together, unimpressed.

"And now, just now, you think your husband's collecting child porn videos on the dark web and chaperoning little girls to the park? Come on, lady. Spit it out. I ain't got time for bullshit."

Judy's eyes widened as she slumped back in the booth, her shoulders sagging.

"A few years now," she admitted, barely audible. "I know I should've turned him in long ago, but I didn't know how to do it. I… I…"

Judy started crying, looking down at her seltzer.

For reasons she couldn't explain, she trusted Thomas. Maybe it was the way he didn't flinch. Didn't rush her. Didn't judge.

In less than thirty minutes, she felt safer with this grizzled stranger than she had in her own home for years.

Maybe, just maybe, he really could save her from this nightmare.

Or maybe he was hiding something, too. Something buried deep.

Thieves stick together, after all.

He didn't flinch.

Thomas let her words settle in the space between them like dust after a detonation.

He pulled a small green notebook from inside his windbreaker and flipped to a fresh page.

"So," Thomas said casually, pen poised, "Who do you think the little girl in the park with Marvin was?"

Judy didn't flinch. She knew the question was coming. No lies. No hesitation.

"That's his mistress's daughter," she said. "They work together. He's been keeping them, both of them, for at least two years. Marvin has no idea that I know."

Thomas's pen hovered, unmoving. He looked up, expression flat, a faint smirk tugging at the corner of his mouth.

"And how old is this little girl?"

"Twelve," Judy said emphatically.

"Make, model, and plate number of his car, if ya know it," he said, not looking up.

"The woman at the company, name?"

Judy hesitated, then spoke like she hated the sound of it.

"Stephanie Edmunds."

"She's in logistics or something, her name's on a few emails I've seen when I was snooping."

"Edmunds," Thomas repeated as he scribbled. "The girl's name?"

"Holly. She's got her mother's face. And Marvin's attention.

I followed them once, from a restaurant in Marlton to a shopping plaza in Voorhees, where they met up with Holly's mother. While they were waiting in Marvin's car for Stephanie, Marvin kissed the girl's forehead and cheek. It wasn't... it didn't look right. It didn't feel right."

Thomas finally looked up.

"Why is Stephanie letting Marvin drive her daughter around? Take her to lunch?"

"Marvin told her he could get Holly a modeling gig. Said Nike was casting for a kids' clothing line, and he had connections, on the condition that he could be her manager. Said he'd handle her photos, portfolio, the whole thing. All upfront expenses paid. Stephanie was all about it."

Thomas narrowed his eyes.

"How'd you find that out?"

"I read the emails and some text messages between them," she replied.

"So let me get this straight, you've got motive, intel, and more than enough red flags to blow up this guy's life. But instead of calling a lawyer, you called me."

Judy's voice dropped, laced with cold resolve.

"No lawyer is going to get me into Marvin's vault of money," she said, hostility threading through each word.

He leaned in, pressing his gut against the edge of the table, voice low and firm.

"Your husband is a predator, lady. A fucking pedophile. And God knows what else he's doing at this very moment, if not grooming a twelve-year-old girl for sex, then probably taking all kinds of pics and videos of her with hidden cameras, or while she's asleep in her bed!

And you're sitting here worried about getting his money? That makes you just as guilty," he said in disgust.

Judy snapped back, voice sharp and raw.

"You think I don't know that? I want him dead. I need him dead."

Thomas shook his head slowly.

"I'm not a murderer, lady."

"But if I help you? What then?"

She stared down at the glass in front of her, the condensation puddling like a slow, cold tear on the table.

"He's worth over ten million dead, plus a few more million in assets," she whispered. "I'll do good with the money, Thomas, I swear. Donate to victims. Kids like the ones he's exploiting. He stays alive, he stays protected. And he keeps doing what he's doing."

Thomas leaned back in the booth, tucked his pen and little notepad back into his windbreaker pocket, and folded his arms across his chest.

A half-smirk crept under his eyes, tired and knowing.

"Gimme a couple of days. I'll be in touch. If you really wanna do this…"

Judy started to speak, "How much?"

But Thomas raised a hand, palm out.

"Don't. Not yet. You think you wanna do it now, but sleep on it."

He folded his arms across his chest once again, voice low and steady, a slight New York accent slipping through:

"Ten million on the line? You can afford my rate."

He slid a ten-dollar bill from his pants pocket and dropped it on the table before getting up and walking out.

The door swung outward, hitting the mist of rain just beginning to fall. It sprayed Hawk's face delicately as he stepped into the late noon covered by grey clouds.

The scent of wet asphalt hit him first, sharp, earthy, and electric. It curled into his lungs like a warning. The storm had passed, but the world still felt charged, like the air itself was holding its breath.

He felt it in his chest. Something was coming. Something was about to break the long, uneasy silence that had lingered too long.

He didn't look back.

Judy sat there, alone. One hand traced a slow circle through the puddle beneath her glass. The other wiped at her face.

She wasn't crying. Not anymore.

Her cell buzzed in her jacket pocket. She pulled it out.

A text from Marvin lit up the screen:

"Taking Holly to a photo shoot around 6 p.m. Same location. C U 2NITE."

Chapter 6

The morning sun rose over Cherry Hill, casting a shimmering glow across the manicured lawns and stamped driveways. Birds chirped in the trees. Sprinklers hissed rhythmically up and down the blocks.

All was calm in the tidy, upper-class neighborhood, except for the home of Marvin and Judy Malmuth.

Inside their center-hall Colonial, boasting Doric white pillars and landscaped shrubbery cut into perfect geometric shapes, Marvin stood at the bathroom mirror, dressed neatly in slacks and socks, buttoning his shirt with the deliberate care of a man who liked things just so. He hummed to himself, watching his reflection with a mix of satisfaction and self-assurance.

Judy stepped in, already dressed in her workout attire, tight brown yoga pants, a fitted sports bra, and sneakers that made no sound against the tile floor. The muscles in her arms were taut, her posture coiled with intent. A multicolored butterfly tattoo peeked out from the small of her back, the delicate wings rising and falling with each step.

She was holding a steaming mug of coffee.

She smiled as she watched him struggle with the last few buttons.

"Still can't do buttons without me, huh?" she teased.

Marvin grinned, his tone dripping with playful sarcasm.

"I'm helpless without you. Hey, you look pretty hot, baby."

He rubbed his hands over Judy's bare belly and the small of her back.

"Be careful, Marv. Hot coffee." She set the mug down on the counter, right beside the sink.

"Don't let it go cold, babe," she said, almost too casually, as she squirmed away from his delicate grope.

"You were up late on your computer last night, Zoom call? I heard you talking to someone."

Before he could answer, she pressed on.

"I've gotta run. Jackie signed me up for a new yoga class. Starts at nine. Strictly no latecomers."

Judy leaned in and kissed his cheek. Her lips trembled slightly. Then she was gone, hurrying down the stairs, out the door.

"Yeah. I was on a Zoom meeting," Marvin muttered to himself. Then he called out louder, "Yoga? No thanks."

"Be good today!" Judy's voice echoed.

The door shut behind her.

Marvin picked up the mug and took a long sip. He didn't get halfway through before something shifted inside him. His eyes blinked rapidly. His breath hitched.

He dropped the mug, and it clattered against the sink without breaking.

The world tilted. His legs went soft beneath him, knees buckling. He grabbed for the counter but missed, his arms useless, trembling. He collapsed slowly, guiding himself toward the edge of the tub. As he weakened, he placed his hands behind him, attempting to catch his fall as his body dropped into the large garden tub.

His landing was soft against the faux enamel. He tried to rise, but his muscles no longer obeyed.

A minute later, the bathroom door opened again.

Judy stepped in slowly. Her hands, now wrapped in black latex gloves, trembled as she pushed the door open. Her face was blank, unreadable, as she stared down at Marvin's body, legs draped awkwardly over the side of the tub, twitching.

She crossed the room with methodical steps, calm and clinical.

Leaning over his dying body, she began to undress him.

First, she loosened the tie. Then came the buttons, one by one, the ones she had just buttoned for him. She peeled away the shirt, then tugged off his pants, underwear, and socks.

Without a word, she reached down and pushed the stopper into the drain.

The faucet roared to life under her hand. She turned it on full blast, tepid water steaming as it splashed against the sides of the tub.

Marvin convulsed. She knelt, cradled his head, and carefully maneuvered it under the stream, like she was washing away what he was. The water now poured directly into Marvin's partially opened mouth. He gurgled, eyes bulging in panic.

Turning her head away so she wouldn't see his face, Judy pressed her gloved hands against his chest, holding him down, making sure the water surged into his lungs. Memorized motions from a well-studied plan.

When his body went limp, she stood calmly, holding back her panic. She concentrated.

No hesitation.

She picked up the coffee mug from the sink, dumped what little remained, and rinsed it once. Then again.

Her hands moved with cold, mechanical efficiency, just like Thomas Hawk had shown her.

She wasn't in control anymore. Something else was. Someone else.

Judy gathered Marvin's clothes from the bathroom floor. She folded his shirt neatly and dropped it into the hamper. Then she smoothed out his trousers and hung them back in the closet, creased and ready, as if he might wear them tomorrow.

By the time she backed the white Range Rover out of the driveway, her alibi would already be in motion.

To yoga and back by 10:30 a.m.

Would she be able to keep a calm face in front of Jackie? Or would it slip through, in her voice, her eyes? Would she confess without even realizing it?

These thoughts swirled in her head as she backed out of the garage, her hands trembling on the wheel.

Out of nowhere, a figure appeared behind the Range Rover.

Judy slammed on the brakes. The steady warning beep cut through the radio, a shrill override that jolted her back to the moment.

The seatbelt locked across her chest as the car lurched. The tires gave a short screech on the pavement.

Her heart punched against her ribs as she studied the figure through her side mirror.

She tapped the window button. It rolled down quietly as it

disappeared. Her breath shallowed.

The figure stepped forward through the morning haze, slow and deliberate.

"Can I help you?" she called out, trying to sound casual.

"Put the car in Park, Judy," the figure said, calm, firm, unmistakably authoritative.

Judy froze, recognizing the voice. She pressed her foot harder on the brake and turned the dial on the console to *P*.

As he came into full view, standing beside her car door, her anxiety shifted.

Relief, or something like it, rippled through her.

"Thomas!" she breathed. "What the hell are you doing here?"

"Let's go inside for a minute," he said, without emotion.

"This wasn't part of the plan!" Judy snapped, panic rising in her voice. Her pulse was spiking.

They had gone over everything: poison the coffee, get him in the tub, clean up, leave for yoga, meet Jackie. Alibi airtight.

Still, she trusted him. She had to.

Confused but obedient, she eased the car back into the garage.

The garage door began its slow descent behind them.

He followed her in, eyes scanning every detail, posture coiled like a man who'd seen a thousand ways things could go wrong.

As Judy pushed the car door open with her foot and stepped out, Thomas appeared out of the shadows like a phantom, silent, fast, and focused.

He grabbed her arm with just enough force to maintain control of her movement.

Her eyes widened, not in fear, but in realization.

Shit, Thomas. What's up? What are you doing?

A sudden sharp pain at the base of her spine. Then warmth, as her knees buckled.

Her breath caught in her throat as the world tilted.

She collapsed slowly, almost gracefully, into Thomas's arms.

He caught her, steady and cold.

"Easy now," he whispered.

Judy's eyes widened as she tried to speak. Her eyes were shouting *Why?*, but no words formed from her mouth.

Thomas held her in his arms and carried her into the house.

Up the stairway. Into her bedroom.

He laid her dying body to rest on a bed of satin.

11:30 a.m. The temperature had already climbed to 88 degrees, hotter than usual for this time of year. The Malmuth residence shimmered in the midday heat, its quiet suburban façade interrupted by streaks of red and blue light bouncing off windows and parked cars. Patrol units idled at the curb, engines humming, while crime-scene tape fluttered like a warning in the dry breeze. A dog barked somewhere down the block, setting off another in the distance.

Out front, a woman in her mid-thirties stood barefoot in flip-flops, silky workout shorts clinging to sweaty legs, a black tank top stuck to her back. She trembled, arms wrapped around herself as if to hold her bones together. A Cherry Hill PD officer hovered beside her, speaking softly, one hand resting on her shoulder, guiding her away from the walkway.

Across the street, curious neighbors peeked from behind blinds. A few had stepped onto their porches in robes and slippers, drawn to the scene like addicts to their fix.

Inside, the Malmuth home had become a crime scene. Marvin's body floated motionless in the garden tub, limbs stretched and stiffened, water still rippling around his head. The room buzzed with hushed conversation as a detective, two county crime-scene techs, and HTCU Sgt. Conners snapped photos and jotted notes. Captain Di Angelo arrived and joined Conners, surveying the room with practiced detachment.

"So, Cap, here's what we've got so far," Conners began, flipping open a notepad. "The guy in the tub is Marvin Malmuth. The woman on the bed in the bedroom is his wife, Judy Malmuth. According to officers who knew her, they were local socialites, who made the cover of NJ Magazine last month in the 'Ask the Professional' feature about pharmaceutical drugs."

Di Angelo's voice was low but firm. "Tell me about the guy in the tub."

Conners scratched the back of his neck. "That's Marvin Malmuth. Could be a heart attack… or an overdose. Hell, he might've slipped, hit his head, and drowned. Rundle's working that angle."

Di Angelo's brow furrowed. "And Mrs. Malmuth?" He nodded toward the bedroom.

They stepped across the hall. Conners, about six-feet-two, boots easily a size 12, crept through the plush white carpet toward Judy's body. She lay sprawled across the king-sized bed, partially nude and covered with a blanket. One arm dangled off the edge, fingers limp, as if she'd reached for something, or someone, before everything went dark. Techs rolled her gently, searching for needles or drugs. There was nothing.

Lividity had already begun to set in, dark red blotches blooming across her pale skin, coalescing with the butterfly tattoo at the small of her back. The inked wings seemed to bleed into the pooling blood beneath her skin, turning the once-delicate image grotesque.

On the dresser lay two unopened glassine bags, each containing a blue wax paper stamped **RED DEVIL** in blood-red ink. Di Angelo leaned in. That stamp triggered something; he'd seen it years ago on North Camden raids during his NARCO days. He knew that set well and who used to run it. It was definitely heroin.

"Maybe she got a bad batch? Run field tests on these bags. Fentanyl, maybe?" he muttered, straightening up. Then, louder, he warned the crew, "Watch yourselves around this stuff, don't touch anything without gloves."

"We could be looking at a bad batch." Bad batches of fentanyl were popping up all over the county, and across New Jersey, for that matter. Any cop who heard those words knew what it meant: just breathing it in or brushing against it bare-skinned could drop you where you stood.

He scanned the room again, something gnawing at his gut. "What's that I'm hearing?"

Di Angelo turned to Sergeant Conners, brows narrowed. Conners looked uneasy.

"That's the other thing I wanted to show you before we shut it down…" He gestured toward a laptop glowing on the desk across the room. "It's a video, Cap. Of kids."

Di Angelo rolled his eyes. "Porn?"

Conners nodded. "Yeah. It's a common one we find in child-porn evidence seized on search warrants. You know the 'Vicky' videos? The ones where the girl's dad filmed her having sex with guys throughout her childhood, from about five years old to…"

Di Angelo placed a hand on Conner's shoulder, stopping him. "I'm aware of the videos, Sarge," he said, disgust in his voice.

"Only one video playing?" Di Angelo asked, flat but sharp.

"Yes, sir," Conners replied. "It's on a loop, Cap."

Di Angelo stared at the screen for a moment, jaw tight.

"All right. Don't shut it down; follow full forensic protocol. Charge it before the battery dies and hook it up. I want a full dump of the drive. Every file, every message, everything."

He stepped back, scanning the room one last time.

"Let's find out what the hell these two were really into."

"Sgt. Rundle!" Di Angelo called. Rundle turned from the hallway and smiled. He and Di Angelo touched elbows, a quiet nod to their academy days.

"This one's strange," Rundle said. "No head trauma, no electrocution, no struggle. If he drowned, we'll confirm with water in the lungs. No pills, no drugs, no empty bottles in the bathroom. The M.E. is leaning toward natural causes. Still, we need an autopsy and a tox screen to confirm. They must have had a 'bad batch,' Cap."

"Anyone else live here besides the wife?" Di Angelo asked.

"No, sir," Conners replied, catching the tail end of the exchange.

"Let's take another look at the wife, Cap," Rundle said, enthusiasm creeping into his voice, the kind that comes from years of seeing bodies and distancing the job from life outside work. Rundle lived for this. Once, he peeled the skin off a hand pulled from the Delaware River and slipped it over his own fingers like a glove, just to get a clear fingerprint. He loved stunts like that, especially when they made coworkers and supervisors squirm. The crazier the stunt, the more they left him alone to his craft, all in the name of science.

He crouched beside the bed and pointed. "There's no residue around her nose, so she didn't snort anything. The bags are still sealed; can't find any more in the house so far."

Rundle held the reagents field-drug test kit in his gloved hand. "Let's field-test it," he said, his voice muffled behind his filtered mask. Carefully, he opened one glassine bag, exposing trace yellowish powder. With practiced hands, he swabbed a small amount, sealed it into the plastic pouch, and snapped the ampoule. A faint crack echoed, followed by a slow bloom of color in the testing chamber. The chemicals were mixed with a sharp shake. Seconds later, a single pink line appeared on the test strip, positive for fentanyl.

He glanced back at Di Angelo. "She had to have overdosed, Cap. Not your typical heroin user, no obvious track marks, nothing on the scene, no rig to be found. And her body doesn't have that strung-out look."

Rundle stood, brushing his hands off on his slacks. "She was in shape. Healthy. Hell, a good-looking woman. Love the tramp stamp, too."

He shook his head. "Damn shame." He held up the test kit. "I'll document the findings and send the bags to the lab for confirmation. We'll need toxicology to verify my suspicions, though."

"I'll send this shit to the lab, Cap. Let them confirm the final dispo,"

Rundle added, pulling fresh yellow caution tape from his plastic toolkit and stringing it across the doorway with practiced ease.

"Who was first on the scene?" Di Angelo asked, sharp and direct.

"Officer Morrison, Cherry Hill PD," Rundle shouted from the bathroom. "I think she's still with the caller." He stepped out and leaned toward Di Angelo's ear, dropping his voice to a conspiratorial murmur. "The hot one in the tiny shorts and tight tank? Damn, Cap, she's got me thinking bad thoughts." He snorted, lifted his eyebrows with a smirk, and walked off toward the bedroom like he was clocking in at a construction site, unbothered, mechanical.

Di Angelo allowed himself a brief smile. "Yeah," he muttered. "I spotted her when I pulled up." He shifted gears. "Any cameras on the house?"

"BLINK system," Conners answered. "Doesn't look like it was activated. No lights, no alerts."

Di Angelo frowned. "Check the neighbors. Somebody around here's got security. This is Cherry Hill, it's crawling with nosy neighbors."

"I already talked to the folks on the right as you pulled in. They've got a Ring cam, but the angle's no good. It doesn't catch the Malmuths' walkway or garage."

Di Angelo gave a short nod and stepped onto the front porch. The morning air was thicker now, hotter, the sun climbing higher, spotlighting the chaos. He walked down to the sidewalk where Officer Morrison was still talking with the woman in the black tank and shorts. Morrison turned as he approached. A fifteen-year veteran of CHPD, she kept her voice low and steady, but her eyes were alert and curious.

"Hi, Captain," Morrison said. "Good to see you again, just wish it wasn't under these circumstances."

Di Angelo nodded, expression tight but familiar. They had a good history from working together on the Internet Crimes Against Children Task Force. Morrison had been one of the best in the unit, fearless in the field, brilliant at roleplay, and relentless in pursuit of predators. Dozens of sting operations, countless arrests, some leading to entire pedophile rings and dark-web distributors getting taken down. From Jersey to Seattle, Morrison left a trail of closed cases and locked-up predators. Di Angelo respected her more than most.

Stepping away from the woman, the two exchanged a quick hug.

"Cap, the woman's name is Jackie Gavin," Morrison said. "She called it in." Said Judy, Judy Malmuth was one of her best friends in the neighborhood. They've known each other for a little over a year and were supposed to meet for yoga this morning." She paused. "Judy never showed. At first, Jackie didn't think much of it; she figured she had gotten held up. But after class, she started texting and calling. No response." Morrison flipped open her notepad. "Jackie said Judy told her that she and Marvin had been going through some issues. Jackie figured maybe they'd had a fight and Judy just needed space." She nodded toward Jackie.

"I'll give you an intro," Morrison said. They walked over together.

"Jackie, this is Captain Di Angelo, Camden County Joint High Tech Crimes Task Force," Morrison said gently.

"Hello," Jackie replied in a low, shaky voice. Her eyes were red and swollen, tissues clutched tightly in her hands, now balled up and frayed from overuse.

"Hi, Jackie," Di Angelo said softly. "I know this is hard, and I hate to make you go through it again. But I need to ask you a few important questions, okay?"

"I understand," she whispered.

Di Angelo pulled a small notebook from his suit jacket, opened it, and flipped through the pages. On one was scrawled in hurried pen: **Key?** Beneath it, a single word, **Cell.** He stared at the page, brow furrowed, then shut the notebook without another thought.

"Thank you," he whispered, then shifted his tone, professional, steady. "How did you get inside the house?"

"There's a hidden key," Jackie said, pointing vaguely toward the garage. "Under a flat piece of slate by the door. Judy showed me, once, when she went away, and I took care of her plants. I left it on the little table inside when I went in. It should still be there. There's another one hidden under the deck railing cap out back."

Her answer was clear, calm, and believable. Di Angelo nodded. "Tell me exactly what you did after you placed the key on the table." He slipped the notebook back into his pocket and leaned forward slightly, squinting as if trying to make out words in a noisy room.

Jackie, now a little more composed, took a breath. "I walked in, put the key on the table, and called out for Judy. Then for Marvin. No answer. I looked around, walked through the kitchen into the garage, and saw both their cars parked inside." She paused, eyes distant. "I figured maybe they were having a fight, although I didn't hear anything. Or maybe… they were, you know, together. Intimate. So I decided to go upstairs quietly."

Her voice trembled, breath shallow. "At the top of the stairs, I turned right. To the left are the guest rooms and a hall bath. To the right, their office, and the master bedroom at the end of the hall." She swallowed hard. "I heard children laughing or crying. Couldn't really make it out. I thought, okay, they're watching TV. I knocked on the bedroom door three, maybe four times, softly. Then I opened it and…"

Jackie broke down again.

Di Angelo gave a quick wave to Officer Morrison, who stepped over and handed him a box of tissues. He passed them gently to Jackie, who dabbed her eyes and took a few breaths.

"I'm sorry, Captain," she whispered. "This is so hard. I'm still in shock. I just… I can't believe this."

But Jackie pressed on. "Judy was lying on the bed." Her voice wavered as she tried to mimic her earlier tone. "'Hey, girl, what's up?' I said jokingly. 'You stood me up, bitch! What's up with that? You overslept?" She gave a weak laugh, then shook her head, eyes glassy. "Then I got closer to the bed…and I could see something wasn't right."

Her voice cracked, and tears welled again. She sniffled hard. "She was pale, no, not just pale. Grey. I touched her and she was ice cold." Jackie's hands trembled as she spoke. "I ran downstairs, fast. Out to my car, where my phone was. Called 911." Di Angelo placed a steady hand on her shoulder. Her skin was burning, grief and adrenaline radiating off her like sunburnt skin. "When did you notice Marvin's body?" he asked gently. "I didn't," she said, quickly shaking her head. "I never saw him. I ran out of her room, straight down the steps, and out to my car. I got so scared, I never looked around. The officer told me Marvin was dead too, but… that's it." Then her expression twisted in horror, confusion, and rage. "Did that bastard kill her?! Did he commit suicide? Killed her, then himself?" Her curiosity outweighed the tears. "Judy hated him." She said in a low voice as she sat down on the edge of a large concrete planter between the garage doors. Di Angelo remained silent, letting Jackie talk. She was giving him intimate details about the victims, details he'd have to dig up eventually anyway.

Jackie looked up at Di Angelo. "She was planning on getting divorced. I gave her a number to a Private Investigator to spy on him. He was definitely cheating on her."

"How do you know he was cheating on her?" Di Angelo fired back.

"Well, I never saw it, but Judy said she had proof and that she was keeping quiet about it till she got her shit in order."

"Do you know if she contacted the PI?" Jackie shook her head.

"No. I believe she decided against it. She was going to contact an attorney instead."

"Do you have the name and number of that Private Investigator?"

Di Angelo asked. "I do. It's in my cell. I can give it to you."

"Thanks," Di Angelo said, pulling his phone from the carrier on his belt.

Jackie brought up the contact and held out her screen. Di Angelo snapped a quick photo. The contact's name read: **Hawk PI**. His stomach tightened. **Hawk.** Could it be? Thomas? "Can't be," he thought. Still… it hit like a punch. "Got it," he said, forcing calm.

Di Angelo smirked slightly and thanked Jackie for her time. He handed her his card. "A detective from the county will be following up with a few more questions. If you know any next of kin or come across anything you think would be useful in this investigation, here's my contact info." He tapped the card. "My office cell is on the back, just in case you need anything or remember anything you think might help our investigation."

Chapter 7

The morgue was cold. Fluorescent lights buzzed faintly overhead, casting a sterile glow across stainless steel surfaces. The air reeked of antiseptic, but beneath it lingered the inescapable undercurrent of death, a metallic scent that clung to every corner. Two examiners stood over Marvin Malmuth's dissected body. He lay on a steel table, wrinkled, pallid, and slightly bloated. His hands rested palm-up, fingers slightly curled, frozen in a state of half-surrender.

The medical examiner, gloved and methodical, dictated into a handheld recorder without breaking rhythm. "This is Medical Examiner Dr. Chris Cabana, Tri-County Medical Center, located at 1900 Cooper Hospital Morgue Unit, Camden City. White male, forty-eight years of age. Approximately five feet," he glanced down at the table, checking the notes from the forensic investigator, "five feet, nine inches tall. One hundred eighty-eight pounds. Decedent was found deceased in a bathtub this morning, approximately five hours ago." He checked his watch. "The time is approximately 3:00 p.m."

He lifted one eyelid, noting the opaque, clouded cornea, then examined the torso. "The decedent was submerged in water."

The first cut, the classic "Y" incision, had already been made by his assistant, Lynne. She was a postmortem technician, new to the field, but had been working with Dr. Cabana for a few months. Still, she'd probably made more "Y" incisions than most techs with years in the business. There was no shortage of dead bodies in Camden.

Dr. Cabana examined the organs now exposed. "Autopsy findings include overexpansion of the lungs, frothy fluid in the airways, and water in the stomach." He gently touched the fingertips, observing the skin. "Wrinkling of the epidermis, suggestive of prolonged immersion. No marbling of the skin, no decomposition. The body wasn't in the water for very long."

The examiner paused at the neck. He leaned in. "No ligature marks, no petechia, no contusions or hemorrhaging found on head or body that would be consistent with a fall or bludgeon-type of force."

Lynne moved to the top of the table and began making a circular incision around the decedent's scalp, carefully exposing the skull. Cabana stepped beside her, holding a small electric oscillating saw. "Want the honors?" he asked, handing it over. Without hesitation, the technician began cutting into Marvin's dead skull. Fine particles of bone drifted into the air, skull dust swirling under the harsh glare of the fluorescent lights, suspended until the slightest breeze altered their direction, causing them to slowly drift to the floor.

Cabana pressed into the throat while Lynne was removing the brain. He was half-expecting cartilage to crunch as he probed with his fingers, but it didn't. The trachea was undisturbed. "No evidence of crushing or structural compromise to suggest some type of strangulation."

Most of the autopsies in this office involved either homicides or accidental overdoses. So, when the usual obvious signs weren't there, when things didn't add up to one of those scenarios, Dr. Cabana felt it in his gut. It made him think he'd missed something. And that surprised him.

"Examination of the heart showed no blockage or narrowing of coronary arteries, ruling out a heart attack," Dr. Cabana continued. "Brain examination shows no signs of bleeding (hemorrhagic stroke) or areas of infarction (ischemic stroke). No clots or blockages of the cerebral arteries, and no signs of emboli or atherosclerotic plaques. Slight Cerebral edema."

A long pause hung in the air as he watched his assistant scribble notes. "Preliminary cause and manner of death: asphyxiation by drowning. Awaiting on tox." He reached over and clicked off the recorder with a soft click that punctuated the silence. Peeling off his gloves with honed precision, clearly a man who'd done this too many times, Dr. Cabana muttered under his breath, "Guy was healthy. Healthy people typically don't die in this manner. Drowning in a bathtub?"

He looked over at his assistant. Behind her mask, a soft voice asked, "Nothing suspicious, Chris?"

"That's what's so suspicious, Lynne." He peeled off the last glove and sighed. "Contact the County. We're calling it a drowning for now. Cause: Drowning. Manner: Accidental. Awaiting Tox."

There was another body a few feet from Marvin's dissected remains, covered in a white sheet, his wife, Judy.

Dr. Cabana approached and slowly lifted the edge of the sheet. She hadn't died in the tub with him; that was clear to him. Judy's skin was smooth. Her body, toned and lean. Cabana had seen bodies like this before, homicide victims whose exterior gave little away. The kind of cases where a bullet left a single, fatal mark while the rest of the body looked... untouched. That's what this felt like. Untouched. From what he could tell with a quick visual exam, there were no bruises, no abrasions, no obvious trauma.

"What happened to you, young lady?" Dr. Cabana said aloud as he put on a fresh pair of gloves. He glanced at the wall clock. The second hand ticked like a metronome. "Lynne, let's take a few extractions."

His assistant uncapped a long needle and handed it to the doctor. He pushed it gently into the soft tissue just below Judy's sternum. He knew the exact angle to pierce the pericardial sac. A few milliliters of clear fluid were pulled back into the syringe. No blood. No effusion. Heart failure is unlikely. Next, he drew a small sample from her femoral vein; if any drugs were still circulating, the tox screen would tell. Finally, with a gloved hand, he gently rolled back her eyelid and took a vitreous tap from the corner of her eye. The thick gel would be stable; glucose, potassium, and other chemicals would leave their traces there.

"Damn." She looked healthier than her husband. "Where'd they say she was found?"

Lynne walked over to her desk and pulled out a clipboard full of handwritten notes. "Decedent was found nude, lying on her back in bed, partially covered with a tan bedspread. Decedent revealed some lividity on the backside of her body. No signs that she was moved or placed in the found position. No puncture wounds or obvious signs of trauma. I'm reading Detective Rundle's notes from the crime scene, Doc." Lynne said as she continued deciphering Rundle's handwriting.

"Appeared to have died in bed." Was the last notation on the crime scene report. Dr.Cabana's, eyes narrowed slightly. "Cause: Pending. Manner: Pending. This is one for toxicology."

A moment of silence filled the room as Dr. Cabana glanced once more at the clock. The overworked pathologist was no exception to the system's fatigue. He had more bodies to examine, and just like always, the game was on: homicide detectives wanted their cases ruled "natural," while major crimes preferred their "naturals" reclassified as homicides. Everyone played the push-off game. It was no different in the morgue; if there were no obvious signs, you did the preliminaries and pushed it off to toxicology.

"Let's wrap it up," Dr. Cabana said, peeling off his mask and gloves with a snap. His eyes flicked toward Lynne. "Hey, you wanna try that new Thai place in Haddonfield? Heard it's supposed to be good."

Just like that, the bodies he'd cut open, poked, and examined faded from his mind, like flipping a switch from work brain to after-hours mode. He pulled his cell phone from his front pants pocket and searched for "Lotus Pavilion." Up came the website. He studied the restaurant's menu with more intensity than he'd given Judy's lifeless corpse.

Lynne raised an eyebrow. "Bit pricey, I heard."

Cabana shrugged. "Yeah, but what the hell," he said, rolling Judy's body into a temperature-controlled white box for safekeeping.

Lynne followed with Marvin's corpse and parked the tables side by side. She smiled. "Sure. Why not? Thai sounds good." She said as she closed the large freezer like door behind her.

Chapter 8

The morning was deceptively calm in the quiet New Jersey suburb. A soft breeze rustled the trees lining the street. Inside Allen Hanlon's modest home, the smell of freshly brewed coffee filled the kitchen. There was a knock at the front door. The door was new, made of steel, with no color, just a coat of grey primer. No signs of debris remained from a little over three weeks ago when a team of Entry guys shattered the old one into pieces.

Hanlon answered it in joggers and a T-shirt, a steaming mug in hand. He looked groggy, suspicious, but not alarmed. The man on the doorstep smiled warmly, holding a leather folio under one arm.

"Good morning, Mr. Hanlon. My name is Thomas Hawk. I'm a Behavioral Therapist with Dynamic Healthcare. I've been hired by your attorney, Harold Slovin. I appreciate you letting me drop by. I know you were scheduled for next week, but I had a shift in my schedule. Your attorney said he spoke with you, wanted to get ahead of things?" Thomas rambled like a telemarketer.

Hanlon blinked. "Oh yeah... I thought we were meeting at your office next week? We're doing this here?"

"Yes, sir. I assumed your lawyer and James, your brother," Thomas paused, looking at Hanlon with a squint, "mentioned they prefer in-home sessions for privacy. My office is shared with other therapists and their clients; it gets... busy. But if you'd rather meet there, I can call Slovin and…"

Hanlon shrugged, slipping a hand into his pocket and curling his fingers around his phone. "Nah. Every time I call him, the meter starts. Uh, what'd you say your name was again?"

"Thomas," the therapist in disguise replied.

Hanlon pressed on. "I don't see why I need rehab for something I can explain."

"Well, Mr. Hanlon, I've been advised of your case and the evidence against you. We need to demonstrate to the judge that you're working on and addressing certain proclivities, specifically, the material found on your cell phone…"

Hanlon cut him off mid-sentence. "Right. For the record, though, these charges are baseless. That's straight from my attorney's mouth and my good friend, Congressman Steven Arnold. You also mentioned my brother, so you know I have people who can make this right. Who did you say you were with?"

Thomas offered a sympathetic look. "Dynamic Healthcare." He was aware of Hanlon's politically powerful contacts and the bad press currently circulating in the news and tabloids regarding his relationship with the Supreme Court Judge. Congressman Arnold had skeletons of his own. He was under investigation for covering up crimes and racketeering in the steel unions. Another crooked Jersey politician. Was there any other kind? Thomas thought to himself.

"Still... public scrutiny's a different beast. I'm here to help with the fallout. Keep it quiet. Keep it controlled. Make the public eye see the real you. It's better if we get out in front of this thing before the press catches more wind of this case and pending charges." The therapist paused, then added, "I work exclusively for Mr. Slovin. Trust me, we know how to handle your case. You work for Crown Financial, right?"

Hanlon stepped aside, gesturing for the therapist to enter. "Yes. That's correct," Hanlon answered as they moved through the foyer toward the kitchen. "Have a seat. Coffee?"

"Sure. Thanks," the therapist replied, choosing his seat carefully, angled just right to observe Hanlon as he moved through the kitchen, preparing the cups. "Is there anyone in the house besides you, Mr. Hanlon?"

"No," Hanlon said, not looking up. "My house cleaner comes later this afternoon. Unless she quits on me. My wife, Dawn, left me. Took the kids to her parents' place in Georgia. Can you believe that shit? Georgia. But it's temporary. I'll get 'em back. You watch."

Hanlon turned his back to get a cup from the cabinet above his sink. Thomas swiftly took advantage of the moment, moving in complete silence. He reached into his leather folio resting on the table next to Hanlon's coffee cup. From the folio, he retrieved a slim plastic syringe and removed the cap, revealing a fine, polished needle. He slid it into the black coffee and slowly pressed the plunger. No sound. No splash. Just a quiet stream of clear fluid merging invisibly with Hanlon's dark roast coffee that he had just set down on the table.

That was the beauty of a syringe. It could deliver its poison like venom from a cobra's mouth, liquid poison without puncturing the skin. Or, it could be used like a tiny dagger: a silent stab, precise and intimate enough to let your prey feel the moment death kissed their skin and fed off their blood.

"Here you go," Hanlon said, setting a fresh cup of coffee in front of Thomas.

The two men sat back in their chairs. Hanlon took a long sip from his coffee, exhaled through his nose, and leaned back a little more.

"What did you say your last name was?" he asked.

"Hawk," the therapist replied, watching him closely. "Coffee's good. Thanks."

Hanlon nodded and adjusted himself in his kitchen chair. He attempted to reach for his phone, still in the front pocket of his loose-fitting joggers.

"Have we ever met? I feel like we've met." Hanlon's hand twitched. He missed his pocket. A subtle frown crossed his face.

"Not formally. But I was in the courtroom the day of your hearing. Maybe you saw me there? I spoke with your attorney," the therapist said assuredly.

"Ah, maybe? I thought your face looked familiar. You look more like a hitman than a therapist." Hanlon giggled softly. "Is it warm in here?" muttered Hanlon, clearing his throat.

The therapist tilted his head. "No. You okay?"

Hanlon pushed his chair back and stood, but staggered, grabbing the edge of the counter to stay upright. His face paled. "Just a little... dizzy."

Thomas rose with him, calm and controlled. "Mr. Hanlon?"

Hanlon tried to speak, but his jaw trembled. "My... arms. I can't..." Then he collapsed.

Minutes later, the master bathroom filled with the sound of running water. Hanlon, barely conscious, twitched as the therapist, now wearing black latex gloves, dragged his limp body toward the tub, where he undressed Hanlon.

The water level rose steadily. Steam twisted in the air. No struggle, just fading breath. He was light and puny, as he lifted Hanlon's limp, naked body to his death pool. Thomas lowered him gently into the tub, cradling his head softly as he placed it under the stainless faucet for his final rest. He leaned in, inches from the dying man's face. Dropping his disguise, Thomas Hawk whispered, "For the record, I'm not a therapist and even if I was, therapy wouldn't fix your problem. Now, only God can drop your charges, not your attorney, not your Supreme Court Judge brother, and not your piece-of-shit political friend, Arnold."

Thomas turned the faucet lever slowly as he watched the water surge into Hanlon's mouth and nostrils. His eyes bulged with panic as he held him down, one steady hand pressed against his narrow chest like the weight of a millstone, keeping him submerged. The child pornographer's eyes fluttered beneath the clear water, wide and frantic. While Thomas was completing his mission, he thought, "One less problem for innocent children in the world, especially Hanlon's own two children. One less predator defiling God's perfection. They were spared. One day, they'd understand, their father's death was a gift."

Hanlon lay still beneath the cold, silent surface. Thomas rose slowly, stepping over sweatpants, underwear, and a crumpled T-shirt scattered across the floor. He reached into his jacket pocket and pulled out his small calling card. A picture on the front, writing on the back, the kind you'd expect to find at a funeral. The front displayed a peaceful image of the sky breaking through clouds, sunlight spilling over an ocean, and waves gently crashing onto shore. On the back, printed in neat, simple font, was a single verse: Matthew 18:6. He placed the card on the edge of the tub, carefully centered to ensure it wouldn't be missed by whoever found the drowned pedophile. It wouldn't be his wife or his children, Thomas knew that. Maybe the house cleaner, or a well-being check from his brother, after several unanswered calls. He preferred the latter.

He stepped back, his quiet message left behind. As he exited the scene, he turned and took one last glance at his handiwork. "See you in hell. At least my journey there will have been worth it." Then he calmly turned around and walked to the kitchen table. He wiped his prints from his own mug with a dish towel hanging over the oven door handle. He placed the clean mug neatly behind the other mugs in the cabinet above the sink, peeled off one glove, and placed it in his folio, then zipped it closed.

No panic. No rush. He gave a quick double-take around the house as he exited the front door, grabbing the handle with his gloved hand. "Thank you, sir! Have a great day!" Thomas called out, just loud enough in case someone was walking their dog or the mailman happened to be cutting across the lawns. No one was around. As he closed the door behind him and walked down the pathway to the pavement, he slid off his other glove and stuffed it into his jacket pocket. At the corner, he reached a black Audi, climbed in, adjusted the rearview mirror, checked for onlookers, and drove away.

It was close to 7 p.m., when Detective Rundle called. Di Angelo was having dinner with his wife, Ann, a steady presence in his life since their freshman year at Villanova. Her long black hair framed a face with warm, almond-shaped brown eyes that gave her a distinctly European look. Whenever they traveled abroad, whether through Europe or South America, it wasn't uncommon for locals to mistake her for one of their own. That illusion usually held up… until she spoke. Then her unmistakable South Jersey-Philly accent broke the spell.

The two met during their freshman year. Ann's dorm was on the opposite end of campus from Dominic's, but fate, or maybe boredom, brought them formally together at a campus social one night. Di Angelo had noticed her before. He heard others call her Ann, but had no idea what her last name was. When he first noticed her, he wondered if she was Italian or Spanish; no accents gave her identity away. They shared one elective: Behavioral Psychology. It was known as an easy "A," though Di Angelo ended up with a "C," after forgetting to turn in one of just three required papers. The professor, well into his eighties, spent more time reminiscing about his college days than actually teaching Behavioral Psych.

It didn't take long for Di Angelo to fall hard for Ann. After just one conversation the night of the "Wildcat Social," a conversation that lasted through the entire event and stretched three hours beyond, they both realized they shared more in common than expected: both Italian, for starters. Her last name was Giacoppo, and for Di Angelo, that was a big score. Not that any other nationality would have deterred him, as he already wanted to marry her and was thinking about what their kid would look like, but mostly for two reasons: food and tradition. His family, like most Italians, believed good food and wine could fix anything. Whether it was a wedding, a hospital visit, or a funeral, the table was always full. Plus, she'd already be used to a little shouting, the lingering scent of fried food, and the chaos of holidays, especially Christmas Eve, when the Feast of the Seven Fishes was non-negotiable. Dating an Italian girl also meant easier intros to his father and Aunt Gia, no cultural explanations needed.

The two were also lovers of sports and old movies. Ann had been born in South Philly but moved to South Jersey at fourteen when her parents, hoping for a safer environment and better schools, decided to cross the bridge to the Jersey side. Her dad was a real estate attorney and still had his own practice on the other side of the Ben Franklin Bridge.

As the two began dating, he grew a genuine fondness for her father. Although their politics differed in some ways, they got along and shared a love for the Philadelphia Eagles, Sunday dinners, and Sunday football games in general. They dated all four years of college without ever breaking up, not officially, not even during the rough patches. After graduation, Ann returned home while Di Angelo entered the police academy. For the next twenty-eight weeks, they saw each other only on Saturdays and part of Sundays.

One rainy night, still just a cadet, Di Angelo proposed to her. He had never doubted that Ann was the one; he knew he would marry her from their first conversation. Ann, on the other hand, had dreams of traveling after college, maybe even following in her father's footsteps and attending law school. He didn't care when the wedding happened. When he proposed, he told her there was no rush; he just needed her to know she was the only one for him. She said, "Yes," thankful that he understood her need for space and time. Six months into his law enforcement career, they were married.

Ann always knew when something was bothering her husband. After all they'd been through, she could read him without a word. They had shared the highs and lows, a house, cars, good friends and family, and a beautiful daughter they named Gemma. Dominic brought home challenges from the job: busted knees, back surgeries, bullet wounds, even a manslaughter indictment from the time he killed a drug dealer in self-defense, while deep undercover. If found innocent, he'd be pulled off the streets because his cover was blown. Guilty, he'd find himself in jail with all the other drug dealers he had locked up.

Additionally, during that time, he'd received no support from the newly appointed Attorney General, who rapidly created a reputation for siding with the bad guys and punishing the police. Which only added to the young couple's pressures. Thankfully, after six long months of uncertainty, the grand jury returned a "No Bill." Still, the wait had been agonizing, as they wondered where their fate would lead.

They had weathered it all together. Ann couldn't wait for the day when his cell phone, the one on his hip or the second one tucked in his pocket, didn't ring in the middle of the night, or when she could simply ask him where he'd been without the answer involving a dead body or some other unspeakable crime. They both longed for the day he could retire, sell the house, and move to Pittsburgh, where their daughter had gone to college and fallen in love. She married a nice guy, acceptable, though closely scrutinized by her father on a near-daily basis. Ann had been dreaming of a grandbaby from the moment the two got hitched. But Gemma, like her mother at that age, felt the need to travel, wanted to live a little selfishly for a while, build her career, and hold off on motherhood. There was time. She was young, and the world was tough enough without caring for a baby.

Dominic missed her every day and would love to live close to her once again. But he always knew Gemma was an adventurer, someone who marched to her own beat. Besides, he still had at least half a year left in his law enforcement journey, stuck in this shithole of a place until his pension kicked in fully. He was just glad Gemma had found somewhere better, and a career far removed from guns, murder, drugs, and the kinds of heinous crimes that haunted his every waking hour. Ann's too.

A bottle of wine stood half-finished on the table. A glass of bourbon waited at his right hand. His phone buzzed. He answered without checking. "Hello." His eyes turned up to the ceiling.

"Sorry to bother you, Cap," Rundle said.

"Yo, Run. What's up?"

"Thought you'd want to know where I'm at." A pause. "Allen Hanlon's house."

Di Angelo blinked. "Hanlon? Why?"

"He's dead," Rundle said flatly.

Di Angelo leaned forward, his voice rising just enough to turn a few heads in the restaurant. "Dead? Suicide?" he blurted, the words hitting harder than he intended. He'd seen it before; defendants like these either took their own lives or tried to when the walls closed in.

Across the table, his wife raised an eyebrow. "Dom, lower your voice, hun."

Rundle's voice was low and steady, edged with something heavier. "We're not sure yet. He's floating in his bathtub. Sound familiar? Same setup as the Malmuth investigation. Looks like a heart attack, maybe slipped and went under." Another pause. "And Cap... the Chief wants us to take prints and bag up everything from the bathroom. Get a closer look."

Di Angelo stayed calm, his voice even. "Who called it in? Dawn Hanlon?"

"Really? I thought there was a court order in place?"

"There is," Rundle responded. "The woman who cleans his house is the one who found the body."

Di Angelo could hear Rundle flipping through his notes. "Ida. Ida Doukas. Older Greek lady. She said she knocked on the front door, but no one answered. When she tried the knob, it opened. She said she called out for the Hanlons, but no one answered. So, she started her routine. Cleaned the kitchen, then went to start the bathrooms. That's when she got her surprise. She said she didn't touch anything, ran out of the house, and called Dawn Hanlon. Apparently, she had no idea what the hell was going on with the two. Looks like he's been in there at least half a day. Dude's starting to puff up."

"Anything look off in there?"

"Not really," Rundle replied. "Well, there was a holy card on the edge of the tub. Maybe he was reading it before he kicked? I don't know?"

Di Angelo frowned. "Holy card?"

"Yeah, you know... the kind you get at a funeral."

He ran a hand through his hair. "Was there a picture on it?"

"Yeah. Ocean scene on the front. Prayer or verse on the back. I think it said 'Matthew' ... stand by, yeah, Matthew 18:6."

That one hit like a punch to the gut. Di Angelo stood from the table, touched his wife's shoulder gently, signaling he'd be back in a minute. "Take a photo of the card and send it to me. I want to see exactly what we're talking about."

"Copy that, Cap," Rundle said. There was a brief silence on the line, then Rundle continued, his voice more serious now. "Hey, before you hang up…I don't know if it's just a coincidence, but in the past couple of months, we've had two middle-aged men found floating in bathtubs. Both have something to do with kiddie porn. No forced entry into their homes. If the M.E. rules this one a drowning too, and there's no heart issue or positive tox…" He let the words settle. "We might be looking at a serial killer."

Di Angelo's voice dropped. "Keep it low-key for now, Run. Let's wait on tox for the Malmuths. There was no holy card there, right?"

Rundle responded, "Not that I was aware of, Cap."

"When we get that tox report, we'll know what direction this thing is moving in." There was a short pause between the two. Then Di Angelo said dryly, "God, I hope there's no connection."

"Fingers crossed. Talk soon, Cap," Rundle said as he hung up.

Di Angelo ended the call, but the weight of it stayed with him. "What the hell?" he said softly to himself. He went back to his table, where Ann was waiting with a look of concern. Was she going to get to-go boxes, or were they staying for a complete dinner? She never knew when his phone went off. Tonight, the chicken picante sat untouched on his plate, the bourbon glass in front of him catching more attention than the food. Ann watched him over the rim of her wineglass, letting the silence settle before gently prodding.

"What's going on, Dom?"

He looked up, almost surprised by the question, then gave a small shake of the head. "Just a long week."

She arched an eyebrow. "Bullshit."

A soft smirk tugged at the corner of his mouth, but it faded just as quickly. He leaned back in his chair, rubbing a hand down his face. "Another drowning. Same as the last."

Her eyes narrowed. "Same as that Marvin guy?"

He nodded slowly.

"In the bathtub?" Ann questioned.

"The Allen-Hanlon lockup. He was naked in his bathtub. Apparent drowning. The maid found him. Rundle said he found a holy card, you know the kind you get at funerals?" Ann shook her head, slightly intrigued. "He found it on the edge of the tub."

Ann responded softly, "Maybe he found Jesus? You've had several of these types that kill themselves when they get caught, hun. Maybe his guilt got to him? You told me these types can't be rehabilitated, didn't you? Who the hell knows what was going through his mind? He must have taken some pills and laid in the tub till he drowned. Like the Godfather tub scene." Her eyes widened, her voice excited.

Dom chuckled. "That guy slit his wrists, babe, and bled out."

Ann replied, "You know what I mean, Dom." Ann exhaled. She didn't need the details. She never asked for them. But she knew. And it was that knowing, the burden of it, that bound them together more than anything else. "You think he was murdered? Maybe the maid did it, Dom?" He couldn't tell if she was joking or serious.

"I don't know yet, babe," he said. "Rundle mentioned 'serial killer.' We don't get many of those around here. It'd be a first for me, if he's right." Dominic's thoughts drifted to the Malmuth deaths, that laptop sitting open on the dresser playing the "Vicky" video over and over on a loop. A dead woman is lying naked in a bed. A man's body was floating lifeless in the tub. He kept replaying the scene in his head, over and over. What did we miss? What else was on that laptop? What purpose did it serve? He felt himself slipping, drifting deeper into thought.

Ann reached across the table, laying her hand over his. Dominic came back to reality. "Then be smart. And be safe. You've already given enough to this county and this career! Let someone else handle this one, D. Push it off to another unit like everyone else does, for once!" Ann was showing her resentment for all the times her husband had to answer the call, never called out sick, and never refused an order.

"The office is shorthanded, babe," he said with a sigh. "We've got detectives spread thin across five different units, barely keeping their heads above water. The High-Tech Crimes Task Force is a specialty unit. My unit. That's why I get away with being so involved with these cases. It's a Joint Task Force designed to alleviate some of the workload. Camden City's off the hook with crime, and it's bleeding into the surrounding towns." He paused, running a hand over his unshaven face. "Thank God Gemma is out of this area."

He looked at his wife, those deep, almond-shaped eyes that had seen so much, reminding him of where they started and everything they'd survived. Gemma had the same eyes. "I know I need to spread the wealth a little more and put someone at the lead so I can retire," he added, his voice low. "I'm sure it's killing me slowly...but I'm not dead tonight." He raised his glass of bourbon.

She lifted her wine in kind. "Chin don," they said in unison. Glasses clinked. A brief moment of peace eased Di Angelo's mind.

Later that evening, Di Angelo lay in bed, eyes open, staring at the ceiling as his mind refused to shut down. *Matthew 18:6.* It was his thing. His silent ritual. Whenever they hit a house crawling with child porn or served a warrant on a suspected pedophile, he'd find a Bible, if there was one, and flip straight to that verse. *Matthew 18:6.* He'd highlight it. Sometimes underline it twice. A quiet act of defiance. Of judgment.

His team was aware of it and even joked about it. If someone spotted a Bible during a search, they'd call out, "Yo, Cap, got one for you," and move on. It had become routine, his signature. Like Zorro, but instead of carving a "Z" with a blade, he used a highlighter, marking select words from scripture to send his message.

But now… someone else had used it. Same verse. Same quiet threat. Coincidence? Or something far more intentional?

His body tensed with unrest, legs twitching under the sheets. Ann lay asleep beside him, peaceful in the blue cast of the bedroom TV at low volume, playing spa music. He considered waking her just for the comfort of her warm body wrapped together with his, but decided against it.

"Let her sleep," he thought. "At least one of us can."

His insomnia hit hard every so often. This spell had been going on for two weeks and had no end in sight. He gently removed the covers from his body and swung his legs over the edge of the bed, clicked off the silent TV, stood, and wandered into the living room.

Maybe an old black-and-white movie, Bogart, Cagney, or one of his favourite Westerns. Anything with Lee Van Cleef usually did the trick. They had a way of quieting the noise in his head. Or maybe... a slow sip of bourbon would do the job. Probably both.

He sat flipping through the channels when a commercial came on, somber music, trembling dogs behind rusted cages, pleading for donations to end their suffering. He quickly changed the channel before another sad, broken-eyed pup filled the screen.

His mind drifted back to the first time he'd ever stepped inside a dog shelter. His first job when he was a kid.

He thought back to those Saturdays, before school ended for summer break. Midmorning on Merchant Street outside Dominic's house was already alive with shouts and sneakers pounding on the pavement. The neighborhood kids had gathered, as they did every Saturday, for a heated game of two-hand touch. The first down marker was the telephone pole directly in front of the Webbers' house. Touchdowns? They were scored at the seams where the giant slabs of concrete met, those wide joints like unofficial goal lines.

If the football hit a parked car mid-pass, it was out of bounds. If a kid collided with one during a route? No penalty, just howls of laughter, even if the poor kid limped away holding his bruised elbow or ribs. That was the unspoken rule of the block: pain was temporary, but the game went on.

During the school year, Dominic often came across as a lone wolf, despite having a wide circle of neighborhood friends. But his core crew never changed: Mike, Andrew, Pat, Rob, Vinny, and Joey, all from his block, with a few others drifting in and out over the years.

When they played football in the street, an uneven number of kids meant someone had to be the designated quarterback. That was usually Rob, known as "Bubba" to his closest friends. He had the best arm. Could throw a ball from telephone pole to telephone pole, about 35 yards, with pretty decent accuracy.

On this particular Saturday, Dom was starting his first real job: four bucks an hour at the "Kill Pound," the not-so-affectionate nickname for the "Penn Dog Adoption Center." His shift started at noon, so he still had time to squeeze in a couple of hours of the usual pickup football game.

"I only got till noon," Dom said. "Let's pick teams and get started."

"Yo, Dom!" Mike shouted. "You working at the Kill Pound? Your Aunt "G" hook you up with that gig?"

"Yeah," Dom replied.

Aunt "G", Dr. Gia Di Angelo, volunteered at the township's adoption center. She was 30 years old, sharp, pretty, and every guy in the neighborhood had a crush on her. Didn't matter that she was Dom's aunt, a doctor, or 17 years older than them. A hot chick was a hot chick, and the crew made no secret of how they felt.

"Saturdays and Sundays, twelve to five to start," Dom explained.

"Hours go up in the summer. My father said no moped unless I get a job."

The guys groaned in sympathy. "That really sucks," someone muttered.

"Dom's Aunt "G" is hot, though," Bubba added. "I'd work for her for free. Remember when she came to class and showed us how to dissect that guinea pig?"

"Yeah," Mike chimed in. "She wore a miniskirt. Great legs. Then she threw on that lab coat, and all I could think of was Benny Hill and his sexy nurses."

Those skits were burned into the brains of every young boy, and their dads, too.

"Wait… we dissected a pig?"

They all cracked up, shoving each other and laughing as they split into teams.

After the game, Dominic hopped on his bike and pedaled to 39th Street. He hadn't seen or talked to Thomas since that day at the rectory. A weird silence had grown between them. Never mentioning that day to each other or anyone else.

He parked his bike outside the shelter, took a breath, and walked in. The odour of dog urine and shit smacked him so hard he lost his breath for a moment. He gagged, pulling his shirt up over his nose as he stepped further inside. The sound of barking echoed off the concrete walls, high-pitched yaps mixed with deep, guttural growls. Metal cages lined the walls, some dogs pressing their noses through the bars, others pacing in anxious loops.

Dom was slightly nervous, too, as he looked around for his aunt. As he walked the aisles, being sure not to step in urine that leaked out onto the floor from the pens, he looked up and spotted Thomas toward the back, wearing rubber gloves and a beat-up Phillies cap, hosing down one of the runs.

His Aunt Gia stood nearby, clipboard in hand, speaking with a middle-aged couple eyeing a black lab mix through the fence. Thomas looked up and froze for a moment when he saw Dom. Not angry. Not surprised. Just… guarded. He gave a quick nod, like acknowledging an old teammate you hadn't spoken to in a while.

Dominic gave a small wave and walked over, sidestepping a puddle of murky water mixed with kibble and something unidentifiable.

"Hey," Dom said, keeping his voice casual. "I didn't know you worked here!"

"Hey! Started today. 8 to 12 shifts, Saturdays and Sundays," Thomas replied, not looking at him as he continued spraying down the kennel.

"You missed another good game. Vinny ate shit trying to catch a pass, slammed right into the bumper of Mrs. Murphy's old Ford Galaxy."

Thomas cracked a small smile, still avoiding eye contact. "Classic Vinny."

A long beat passed between them. Just the rush of water and dogs whining.

"You good?" Dom asked, quieter now.

Thomas paused, shut off the hose, and finally met his eyes. "Yeah," he said. But it was automatic. Unconvincing.

"I didn't mean to, after that day, at the rectory…" Dom trailed off. "I didn't know what to say."

Thomas's expression didn't change. But there was something behind his eyes, a quiet aggression. A look in his eye, a look older than someone who was barely a teenager should look.

"I didn't either," Thomas said. "Still don't."

Gia's voice echoed from across the shelter, calling out and waving to Dom. "Hey, Dom, welcome to work!" his aunt shouted down the aisle of barking dogs. "Meet me in the front office and I'll get you set up."

He gave Dom a nod. "Well, my shift is done. Have fun, buddy. It's easy, just smelly. See ya tomorrow, Dom!" Thomas said as he hung his apron up and punched his timecard on the way out the back door.

Dom met his Aunt Gia in her office. She was wearing the white lab coat Mike had mentioned, but no miniskirt. Just bell-bottom jeans, clogs, and a green T-shirt. Her hair was pulled back in a ponytail. She was the cool aunt. His dad's little sister, now a doctor.

Whenever Gia saw Dom, she always greeted him with a hug.

"How ya doin', buddy?" she asked, just like always, as she rubbed the top of his head, her fingers getting lost in his thick black hair.

She knew he was nervous about starting his new job and that he loved dogs.

"This job's a cakewalk, Dom. Just have to keep the kennels clean and make sure the pups have food and water. The smell's the worst part, but you get used to it really quick. We're only opened from 12 p.m. to 5 p.m., so the days go by pretty fast! I'm so happy you're working here! God, you're already taller than me. That's great, I need a big, strong guy around to help with the big dogs! Come on, I'll show you around."

Gia's energy was contagious. She smiled widely at Dom, pausing to look into his brilliant blue eyes with a motherly warmth. Then she grabbed his hand, and together they walked down the aisle of kennels and barking dogs.

She made Dom comfortable and eased his tension, like she had done since he could remember. She always had a way of doing that.

His dad tried, but sometimes fell short in that area. He couldn't, or wouldn't, show vulnerability to his father. Not out of fear. Rather, respect. He knew his father was a hard-working guy and was doing his very best. To show weakness might make him feel like he wasn't doing a good job of raising him.

His father, Jimmy, was a Marine vet and retired State Trooper. Jimmy had taken an early pension after being injured in the line of duty. It happened during a routine car stop. The vehicle had no front plate, and as Jimmy approached, the driver opened fire, shooting him in the knee and chest.

Unbeknownst to Jimmy, the two suspects had just carjacked the vehicle. The owner was already dead, slumped across the back seat. Jimmy never saw it coming. His bulletproof vest stopped the chest shot, but the blast to his knee shattered bone and ended his career. Still, Jimmy managed to return fire, putting two rounds into the shooter, killing him on the spot.

These days, he walked with a limp and kept the pain in check with aspirin and a splash of scotch.

Since the shooting, he'd taken up bartending at his cousin's place, The Philly Tavern, tucked away on Bella Lane near Northern Liberties. It was a rough place to work. A true shot-and-a-beer joint. The crowd was tough, the nights tougher. But Jimmy loved it there. He fit right in.

Jimmy always kept a .38 strapped to his ankle. Everyone in the neighborhood knew "Jimmy D." They respected him, and they knew better than to start trouble in his tavern. If you did, you'd be making a big mistake.

Most mornings, Dom woke to the smell of pancakes, coffee, and bacon. It was a common sight to see his father standing in front of the stove, wearing a white "wife beater" tank top that showed off his USMC tattoo, and black Bermuda shorts. His feet were tucked into a pair of battered bedroom slippers that Dom swore were as old as he was.

It was late morning. Dom and Jimmy had spent most of it catching up on sleep. Outside, a soft rain tapped against the aluminum siding, lulling Dominic into a deeper sleep than usual.

He stirred awake and stared at the clock radio, the black numbers flipping slowly to 11:30. Dom shot to his feet, splashed water on his face, brushed his teeth, and headed downstairs.

Jimmy caught his son's entrance from the corner of his eye and gave him a glance and a crooked smile.

"Grab a plate and sit down, Dom," he said, pointing toward a stack of plates with his spatula, eyes never leaving the frying pan where golden pancakes sizzled.

A pile of bacon rested nearby, wrapped in paper towels, soaking up grease. Jimmy turned from the stove, balancing two perfect pancakes on the spatula, and slid them onto Dom's plate.

"We overslept, buddy. But I was still in the mood for breakfast. Bacon?" he asked, a little too enthusiastically.

"Sure," Dom muttered, rubbing his eyes and stifling a yawn.

Jimmy grabbed his coffee from the stove and sat across from him, creaking into the chair with a grunt.

"Didn't see you last night before you went to bed," Jimmy said, blowing on his coffee before taking a sip. "How was the new job?" He smiled across the table. "Aunt G said you worked hard. Proud of you, son."

"Thanks." Dom shrugged. "It's not that hard. I feel sorry for some of the dogs there. I don't want to see them die or get put down."

He paused for a moment, then blurted out to his father, "Do you ever miss Mom?"

The question landed hard, like a slammed door, loud and sudden in the quiet kitchen. It came out fast, like it had been waiting inside him for years.

Jimmy knew that, as his kid grew older, more talks like this would happen. More information about his time in the Marines, fights, girls, and cars he had growing up, and stories about his mother.

Dom had only been a baby when Jimmy got shot on the job. They never talked about it. If Dom ever asked about his father's limp, he'd get a smirk and something like "hazards of the job" before the subject shifted.

Dom was barely eight years old when he lost his mother, Jenna Mattia. The few memories he had of her were etched deep in his heart and soul.

He remembered the times he'd stay home from school, claiming to feel sick. Like most attentive mothers, Jenna had a knack for spotting the difference between a truly sick child, one pretending to be sick, and the classic Monday morning stomachache. Regardless, there were times she let her desire to keep him home for the day override her layman's diagnosis.

Dominic remembered those days when she would lie beside him in bed, telling stories about her parents, how they came from Italy with no money, barely spoke English, yet somehow managed to open a restaurant in the city. She'd tell him he reminded her of her father sometimes.

If it was snowing outside, she'd pile a mountain of blankets on the sofa, open the blinds, and together they'd watch snowflakes stick to the glass while sipping hot cocoa. Had she known her time with him would be cut so short, she might never have sent him back to school, never let go of his little hand, not for anything. Every day would've been stories, hot cocoa, and snuggles.

Those memories were embedded in him. Whenever snow began to fall, or he saw a couch crowded with soft blankets and pillows, he thought of his mother, and those thoughts sustained him.

Other memories, those Dominic had been too young to retain, were either recalled or reconstructed through stories told by his father and his Aunt Gia. The stories Jimmy told his son were only about the good times they'd shared and the times she held him in her arms till he fell asleep. Nothing of her pain and suffering.

Jenna was beautiful and always watched what she ate and kept the two of them as healthy as possible. She always gave any new diet or workout scheme a shot. She was always in great shape, and Jimmy loved it. He would always tell her she was the prettiest woman in the room, no matter where they went.

Then she started with headaches. Then came the seizures. And then came the diagnosis: gliomatosis cerebri, a rare and brutal brain cancer that doesn't grow in one place; it spreads like a fog across the brain, robbing the body piece by piece. Vision. Speech. Memory. Motor skills.

Six months. That's how long it took for the disease to steal her from them.

Jimmy never left her side. He sat in that hospital room every day, telling her stories, holding her hand, holding a straw to her lips while she tried to sip on water, and feeding her ice chips when that was all she could handle. And then she was gone.

From then on, it was Jimmy and Dom, with Aunt Gia rotating in as the backup quarterback. She was in her final year of veterinary school when Jenna became bedridden. She looked after Dominic while juggling her studies, a backpack full of textbooks and reports slung over her shoulder like a permanent appendage. But Dom always came first, even if it meant pulling all-nighters to keep up with her coursework.

Jenna's family was devastated by her death and didn't pitch in much afterward, not even for Dom. That always made Jimmy angry. Sure, they visited on holidays and birthdays, but that was about it.

Angry, yes, but he also understood. They'd lost their baby. So, he never pushed the issue. He knew he'd manage without them, and he always showed them respect when they did come around.

Jimmy always told Dom stories about her laugh, her patience, and her kindness. The way she used to sing to Dom while rocking him in the fancy glider chair she insisted they buy. It was the latest thing back then, and it gave great support.

Jimmy never got rid of the rocker. It moved from room to room, and to this day it sits in the corner of his bedroom. Never used, but a good place to set his clothes upon. It also served as a constant reminder of the woman he loved. A woman that no other could replace.

Dom looked up from his pancakes, waiting for his father's answer.

Jimmy didn't look surprised. He stared into his coffee for a long moment.

"I always think of your mother. I miss her every day," he said, his voice low. "But I get by because she's a part of you."

He let out a breath and continued.

"The world's a funny place, son. Sometimes it feels like God takes the good and leaves us with the scum of the earth."

Your mom used to say, "God has His plans, and we can't change them." He paused again. "I don't question anymore why God took her. I just tell myself, He had a plan for Jenna. I hope it was a good one."

He didn't say more. He walked to the sink and dumped the rest of his coffee.

Dom immediately regretted asking. He felt the sudden shift in his father's mood; the atmosphere had gone from light to heavy in seconds.

Jimmy was a strong man. Nothing ever seemed to rattle him. If he was scared or sad, no one ever knew it.

Dom quietly finished his meal, then glanced up. "I like a girl named Jasmine!"

The words shot out of his mouth like he was answering a Jeopardy question.

Jimmy turned, a smile creeping across his face. "Do tell, Dom!" The lightness returned to the room. "Jasmine? Jasmine what? Is she hot?"

"Jasmine Dallas," Dominic replied.

He chuckled to himself. Jasmine Dallas. Sounds like a stripper name, or something a porn star would call herself. But his grin widened as he leaned in, eager to hear more. "C'mon, tell me about Jasmine."

Dom laughed and stood up. "She's about this tall," he said, raising his hand to about chin level. "Brownish-blondish hair, green eyes," he added, glancing up toward the ceiling as if picturing her. "Best-looking chick in the joint, Pops," he said, mimicking his father's tone, the way he used to talk about Jenna.

"I gotta get to work. We'll talk later." He shadowboxed a few jabs at his dad.

Jimmy played along, throwing a few lazy punches back in the air. Then he pulled Dom in for a hug.

"Love you, Son. Be careful on that bike."

The sky was dark, the rain just starting to fall as Dom pedaled hard toward the "Kill Pound." He skidded to a stop behind the building, tossing his bike against the rear delivery dock without a second thought. He rushed through the open door, water clinging to his hair and soaking his shirt from the drizzle that felt worse when you were moving fast.

Reaching the grey metal rack, he grabbed his timecard, a bent manila rectangle with his name barely legible in pen, and shoved it into the slot at the base of the old punch clock. A dull thunk echoed as the machine stamped **12:15 p.m.** in faded black ink.

He glanced around, looking for Thomas. No sign of him.

"Hi, Aunt G. Sorry I'm a little late."

"It's okay. I need your muscles." Gia smiled as she brushed a strand of hair from her face. "A shipment of rubber floor mats came in this morning. I can't lift them alone."

She smiled at him again, warmth in her eyes. Dom could do no wrong in her book, not really. And though she'd never say it out loud, the timecard wasn't for payroll. It were just for show, a kind of Big Brother formality to make it all look official. The only eyes it ever saw belonged to her.

As Dom stepped into the loading dock area, he spotted the boxes of rubber mats piled near the wall. Rain had started to soak a few of them, so he hurried over and tried lifting one. They were heavier than they looked; his aunt wasn't kidding. Grunting, he managed to drag the wet boxes closer to the door, out of the rain's reach.

That's when he noticed his bike, completely drenched. With a frustrated sigh, he jumped off the dock and went to move it. Just as he grabbed the handlebars, he caught sight of Thomas pedaling by, soaked to the bone.

"Yo, Thomas!" Dom shouted.

Thomas circled back toward him, tires kicking up a mist from the wet pavement.

"Hey, Dom. We must've just missed each other."

"Gia said they're putting two dogs down today," he said without saying hello.

Dom's stomach dropped. "Seriously? She didn't tell me yet."

Thomas nodded, his eyes tired and distant. "I thought about opening the gates and letting them run. But they probably wouldn't make it past the parking lot. One's blind. The other can barely walk."

Dom hesitated. "Who does it? How… how do they kill them?"

Thomas looked away. "Gia hits 'em with a needle. Poison. Paralyzes them. They die in a few minutes." He paused. "A shipment of the stuff came this morning. I stacked it in the medical closet. Come on, I'll show you really quick."

They moved swiftly through the corridor toward the back. The door to the medical supply closet had a paper sign taped to it: **KEEP CLOSED, VET ONLY.**

Thomas pulled it open slowly, careful not to make a sound, and pointed to a stack of labeled boxes: **SUXAMETHONIUM CHLORIDE**. Inside, rows of tiny vials glinted under the harsh fluorescent light, hundreds of them, neatly packed.

Dom stood quietly, uneasy. Thomas cracked open one of the boxes, pulling out a single vial and holding it to the light. The liquid inside looked pure. Clean. Deceptively harmless.

"Looks like water," Dom said.

"But it ain't," Thomas replied. "Couple drops of this and out go the lights."

Dom glanced nervously at the door. "C'mon, we should get out of here before Aunt G sees us."

Thomas nodded and slid the vial back into its place. They shut the box, then eased the door closed behind them like two kids sneaking out of a forbidden room.

Thomas hopped off the dock and mounted his bike. "See ya later, Dom." He pedaled off, the sky beginning to brighten as the rain let up.

Chapter 9

Sergeant Conners was at his desk when the phone rang. "Conners."

"Hey, Sarge, it's Kimberlee over at the Medical Examiner's Office. I've got those tox reports for you, if you want to swing by and grab them. Maybe we can get lunch if you're here before one o'clock?"

Conners hesitated. "Yo, Kimberlee, that's… awesome."

He did not want lunch with Kimberlee, not because he did not like her; he did. That was the problem. She was likable, smart, and attractive. Too attractive. And Conners, for all his charm, knew better. He played it safe. He knew his limits and had enough discipline and moral compass not to step into a potentially messy situation, like a divorce from his pregnant wife.

From the other side of the room, Silva caught the waver in his voice. She practically leapt toward his desk, grinning like a kid who just caught her big brother singing Shania Twain's *Man! I Feel Like a Woman!* in the mirror when he thought he was alone.

She dropped into a dramatic whisper, mocking: "Oh, please, take me to lunch, honey. Let me be your dessert."

Conners flushed red, his bald head glistening with nervous sweat. He tried to hold back a laugh, swatting Silva away with one hand, the phone still pressed to his ear.

"I'm sorry, Kimberlee. There's no way I can make it up there today. Can you just email me the reports?"

"Sure," she said. "Anything else you need?"

"Yeah, do me a favor. Can you double-check the Malmuth report? Any toxins show up?"

"Stand by, Sarge."

He heard the soft thud of the receiver hitting the desk, followed by the faint rustle of papers being shuffled.

"Okay, let's see…" she muttered, reading aloud now. "Blood, urine, vitreous fluids, gastric contents…" She paused briefly. "All negative, Sarge."

"Seriously? For Malmuth?"

"Drowning, accidental," Kimberlee read off to him. "Yep, completely clean. Judy Malmuth…" There was a longer pause. "Natural. M.E. Doc Cabana signed off as natural."

Conners exhaled sharply. "Thanks, Kimberlee. I really appreciate you."

"My pleasure, anytime. Hope you make it up this way soon."

When Conners hung up, he called out to Silva.

"Yeah, Sarge?" Silva answered from her lab.

"Did you dump the Malmuth laptop yet?"

"Yeah," Silva said. "But I haven't opened the dump yet. Wanna look?"

Conners stood quickly from his desk and headed into Silva's lab.

A rack filled with cell phones sat connected to a forensic computer, each one running software to crack PIN codes. Three large flat screens displayed streams of data from other active cases. Malmuth's laptop rested on a plastic cart alongside several other laptops and digital devices, along with his cell phone. A copy of a data warrant was folded and rubber-banded around it. The warrant had been used to search for Judy Malmuth's cell location and had a five-day limit that had already expired.

Silva plugged in the mirrored hard drive from Malmuth's laptop. She looked a little bewildered.

"There are only three files, Sarge. Three folders. The 'Vicky' video was there, filed neatly in its own folder. But what was found next was even more surprising."

Another folder marked "Medical Contracts." This folder contained several pictures of young girls posing in sexual positions. Some were dressed in pajamas, some in underwear, some nude. Marvin Malmuth was pictured with one of the girls, a young blonde. They were lying naked on what looked like a hotel bed. Silva examined the image carefully. "Someone took this picture, Sarge. This is not a selfie. The angle isn't something he could have taken alone." The little girl appeared to be asleep. Conners felt his stomach twist. "She's drugged, I bet. That's definitely Malmuth." "Wait, look at the window in this picture. There's a reflection." Silva enlarged the image. "It's a female taking the picture, Sarge!" They both looked at each other. Judy Malmuth. Conners's eyes widened. "Fuckin' Judy took the picture. She was completely involved with the trafficking!" Silva scrolled through the images of Judy pulled from the Malmuths' secondary computer found at the scene. She printed a few and laid them beside the blurry reflection. The resemblance was undeniable: same hairstyle, body type, and jawline. The likeness was definitely there. "Take this picture to Agent Negron and have him clean it up."

Silva responded, "10-4. Let's see what this last file has in it." She clicked into the third folder. It was labeled "Millstone." Inside, a single document: The Gospel of Matthew printed over a background of an ocean and blue sky with some clouds. Chapter 18, verse 6 was highlighted in yellow: *If anyone causes one of these little ones, those who believe in me, to sin, it would be better for them to have a large millstone hung around their neck and to be drowned in the depths of the sea.* Conners grabbed his cellphone and quickly dialed Di Angelo's number. "Cap! I got some info for you."

Di Angelo stepped into the squad room and was immediately met by AP Lani and Sgt. Conners. "Hey, Cap," Lani said softly, too softly. Di Angelo caught it instantly. Something was up. Conners offered a curt, "Morning, sir," but didn't move from his spot beside Lani. They were both standing just outside his office door like sentries. Conners handed him a folder. "Just received Hanlon's M.E. report. The ruling is Drowning. Manner: Accidental."

Di Angelo frowned, flipping the folder open. "You've got to be kidding me. Nothing? No substance abuse? Jeez. What the hell is going on?"

"There's something else, Cap," Lani said. Her eyes met his as she tapped the edge of a second file against her palm. Fingernails clicking softly. "Can we talk inside your office?"

Di Angelo didn't answer. He just opened the door and walked straight to his desk, pulling the high-back leather chair out and dropping into it with a heavy flop. Lani and Conners took the two smaller chairs across from him. Lani opened her folder and pulled out the calling card they'd recovered from Hanlon's house. She laid it gently on the desk like it was evidence from a murder scene. "Cap," she said, "this card matches the computer file found on Malmuth's laptop."

Exact same image, ocean, sky, color tone. Everything. We think they're linked." Di Angelo's jaw tightened. "We think we have a serial killer," she added, her voice quieter now. She reached into the folder again and pulled out a photo, a young blonde girl, maybe eleven or twelve. She placed it in front of him. Di Angelo stared at the image, the edges of his vision starting to blur. "Who is she?" he asked, voice low, eyes not leaving the photo. "The girl in the picture lying next to Malmuth has been identified as the daughter of his mistress, Stephanie Edmunds. Her name is Holly Edmunds."

Di Angelo's stomach churned.

Just then, Conner's phone buzzed. "Excuse me, Cap," he said, stepping out of the office.

Di Angelo thought maybe Conners's wife was calling because she was going into labor with their **fourth** child and didn't mind him taking the call. She was due any day. The door clicked shut. Lani stayed seated, her expression shifting, still serious, but tinged with something else. A quiet curiosity. Concern. She leaned forward slightly. "What's up with you and highlighting Bible verses during search warrants?"

Di Angelo looked at her, blindsided. "Who told you that?"

"Detective Morel. I had a trial prep with her. We were talking about HTCU, about the last couple of years... and your name came up. She said the team would go through hell for you."

Lani shrugged, but her eyes stayed locked on his. "I didn't judge it. I figured, hey, if this is your way of keeping your hands off these assholes, go for it. Better than a broken jaw and a lawsuit."

Di Angelo exhaled, leaned back, and was silent for a beat. "You highlighted Matthew 18:6, didn't you?" **"If any one of these**

prosecutors or, God forbid, the Commissioner catches wind of this, they'll make you a suspect, Cap!" Lani warned.

Di Angelo gave her a measured look. "I think you're stretching a little, Lani. I'm not leaving calling cards or laptops." His voice was calm, confident. "And the highlighting? It's discreet. Nobody sees it unless they're looking. Which they are not, because they are too worried about other things, like 20 years in prison." He pivoted quickly. "Let's get back to this, Holly Edmunds girl." It was clear he didn't want to linger on the topic of scripture.

Lani followed his lead. "Turns out Malmuth's mistress, Stephanie Edmunds, lost it when she heard he was dead. Detectives found out he was footing the bill for her condo, on the east side of Cherry Hill."

Di Angelo leaned forward, listening. "They ran his financials, saw the payments, and brought her in. She confirmed they were in a relationship."

"Then," Lani added,

"One of the detectives noticed a picture on her desk. Little blonde girl. Looked just like the one on the Malmuth laptop." She paused. Let it land. "Ms. Edmunds ID'd the girl. It's her daughter, Holly," Lani said.

Di Angelo's brow furrowed. "And what about Mrs. Malmuth?"

Lani shifted in her chair, leaning in slightly. "You spoke with her friend Jackie, right? She gave a formal statement the next day. Swears up and down that Judy Malmuth didn't use drugs, nothing, and we now know the tox report came back negative." She shook her head, gesturing with her hands. "Jackie Gavin, the witness, saw them argue. A lot. And Mrs. Malmuth used to complain about Marvin's cheating. We've got text messages, voicemails on Jackie's cell, solid proof Judy knew about the affairs."

"She knew," Lani said. "About Marvin's other affairs."

Dominic looked up slowly, eyes narrowing. "Agent Negron was able to isolate the image Conners and Silva pulled from Malmuth's laptop. We've confirmed it." She flipped open the folder and slid a photograph across the table. The image was now crisp. The person who took the photo was easy to identify using comparison shots. "It was Judy Malmuth. No doubt about it. She took pictures of Marvin and that little girl, Holly, in bed. Naked."

"We believe Holly is either asleep or drugged, based on how lifeless her body appears in the photos. Her eyes are shut, not like she's choosing to close them, but the kind of shut that looks like deep sleep. And in every shot where she's facing the camera, it's the same." Dominic glanced down. The original photo was captured in dim light. He'd seen CP pics like it before. This one was closer to home. Marvin Malmuth. A guy he had never spoken to. A guy he only saw dead under a few inches of water. The photo brought him back to life. He was shirtless, tangled in sheets with a naked twelve-year-old girl, Holly. The shape of a woman's silhouette. Her reflection, accidentally captured in the glass window, stared back with haunting clarity. It was fleeting, imperfect, but unmistakably Judy Malmuth. His mind flashed back to the crime scene. Her body. Naked, cold, and lifeless, lying in her bed. He stared at it in silence. His jaw tightened, the faintest muscle twitch in his cheek. Then he leaned back, exhaled hard through his nose. "She was documenting it. Judy was part of the game. Or maybe…"

Lani nodded; her voice was low. "Leverage. Or insurance. Or maybe she was making money off it, too? Completely involved in the selling and trading of child pornography or even trafficking."

Dominic rubbed a hand over his face, suddenly feeling the weight of it all. "How long, I wonder? How often did they drug this little kid? Other kids? These people are soulless."

Di Angelo's eyes narrowed.

"What we don't have," Lani continued, "is proof he killed her or she killed him. The crime scene went over that house with a fine-tooth comb. Oh, and get this, still no cell phone for Judy. Even though the GPS last pinged at the house. They checked both bodies. No defensive wounds. No scratches. No bruises. Nothing. He drowned, just like Hanlon. Someone took her cell. There had to be another person in the house, Cap." She let the last line hang. "It's a mystery," she added. "But one thing's not: Mrs. Malmuth was totally involved and knew exactly what her husband was into. Sex trafficking of young girls? Right in your backyard, Cap." She sat back.

Sarcastically grinning slightly, he said, "Cherry Hill scum ain't any better than the scum we got out here, Lani. Probably even worse. At least in this shithole city, you know what you're getting when you get here. You expect it."

Lani sat still, thinking, "Maybe someone drugged them both? Nothing is making sense, Cap!"

Di Angelo grinned crookedly, his forehead wrinkling. "An untraceable drug. One that can fool the tox report." He thought to himself. He'd seen it before. Long before he was a detective. Long before he was an adult.

Chapter 10

Dominic had just left school. It was his turn to dump the trash cans and clap out the erasers. He spotted Thomas heading across the street toward the rectory. Every Friday, Thomas was supposed to meet with Father Asher, part of some deal to pass the class. But, he thought that the deal was over after what had happened at the first meeting. Maybe he and Asher ironed out the whole mess. With only a couple of weeks left before summer break, Dominic couldn't wait for the school year to be over. Maybe then Thomas could start hanging around again.

He jogged over, but Thomas had already slipped inside. The front door was shut and locked. Dominic knocked softly, more out of instinct than intent. He didn't want the other priests, especially Asher, to see him.

Circling around back, he noticed the screen door was shut, but the main door stood wide open. He stepped inside.

The kitchen was dark and still. He tiptoed past the pantry and peeked into the first two offices, left, then right. Empty.

A long hallway stretched toward the front foyer. The door was still locked.

He backtracked, about to leave, when he saw it, a crack of light slipping through a door near the pantry. Barely a sliver.

He moved silently toward it, heart beating faster. Pressed his ear to the door. Nothing.

He turned the knob gently, careful not to make a sound. One step down, no creak. Then another. Confidence growing, he descended the narrow staircase.

As he reached the last few steps, the basement came into view. Damp. Silent. Lit only by a single dim bulb swinging slightly, as if someone had brushed past it moments ago.

Dominic stepped onto the cold cement floor. He scanned the space. A washer and dryer rested on a wooden platform. A utility sink stood against the wall. A metal chair. And near the chair, a pile of clothes?

He walked closer. No. Not clothes.

His legs went numb. His vision tunneled.

Father Asher was on his back. Eyes wide open. Mouth agape. Dead.

Dominic stumbled backward and fell, landing beneath the flickering bulb. His hand hit something small and cold. Without realizing it, he clutched it in a tight fist and scrambled to his feet.

Then he ran up the stairs, through the kitchen, and out the back door.

Three blocks away, gasping for air, he opened his palm. The label read: **SUXAMETHONIUM CHLORIDE** in capital red letters.

His hand started to shake. Dominic knew Thomas had been there. He'd watched him go into the rectory. But had he left when he couldn't find Father Asher? Or had Thomas seen what Dominic had just seen and bolted too?

Or had Thomas killed him?

Did he kill him with dog poison? The thought came briefly, but it stuck.

That bottle, Suxamethonium Chloride, wasn't there by accident.

Dominic needed answers. And he knew exactly where to go: Bethel Cemetery, behind the mausoleum.

He stopped at home first, peeled off his school uniform, and changed into jeans and a T-shirt.

Told his dad he was going for a bike ride.

"Okay," his dad said, grabbing his keys. "I'm headed to work. Dinner's in the fridge. Call your Aunt Gia if you need anything. She'll be by later."

Dominic gave him a quick hug and bolted for the backyard.

"I got it!" he shouted as he mounted his bike and peeled out, standing on the pedals for speed.

Just like he thought, Thomas was sitting behind the mausoleum, chewing on a long blade of grass, tossing stones at a mound of fresh dirt. A new grave.

"Hey, Thomas!"

Thomas looked up, startled. "Hey, Dom! What are you doing here?"

Dominic didn't waste time. He reached into his pocket and pulled out the small bottle, the empty vial of poison.

"Did you?" he asked.

Thomas stared at the label, then laughed, nervously, sarcastically. "Did I what?"

"Did you inject Father Asher with this poison shit?"

"Yeah, Dom," Thomas said, rolling his eyes. "I filled up a needle and gave him a shot. Just like Aunt Gia does with the dogs at the kill shelter." His tone dripped sarcasm, like Dominic was insane.

Then Thomas got serious. He stepped closer, resting a hand on Dominic's shoulder.

"You remember that little kid we saw getting pushed around in the schoolyard a couple of months ago? The one with the accent? Lived with his grandparents who didn't speak English?"

"Yeah. I remember," Dominic said, his voice tight.

"Last week, I saw him leaving Asher's office, not crying, but his eyes were wide and scared, like he'd just seen something he couldn't explain or was told never to repeat. He was shaking. Asher followed close behind, saying, 'It's all about trust, boy. All good. We'll talk again next week.'"

"The kid's grandmother was waiting outside, looking confused. He tried to hide his fear."

"She asked him in broken English, 'Why you shake?'"

"The following week, he was scheduled to meet with Asher. I followed him back to the rectory. But they didn't go into his office. They went to the basement.

I snuck in. Quiet. Careful. They weren't in the office, I checked. Downstairs, in the basement, the kid's pants were pulled down. I could only see his back. His school shirt was on, but his pants were around his ankles. He was just standing there in front of Asher.

Asher was sitting there, staring at him like it was nothing. Like he was watching TV. I heard Asher say, 'Excellent. This is trust.'"

"I panicked. Quietly snuck back up the steps and slammed the door loudly, on purpose. A second later, I heard footsteps thundering up from the basement. And I ran."

Thomas looked away for a second. His jaw clenched. "Right then and there, I decided Asher wasn't going to do this anymore. Not to him. Not to me."

His voice dropped to a whisper. "I didn't inject him, Dom. He drank it. Drank it himself."

Dominic blinked. "What do you mean?"

"I didn't know how I was gonna give it to him. I brought the little bottle, the vial, to school one day, but I had no plan. I had it in my pocket, fumbling with it with my fingers all day long."

"After school, I waited for Father Asher to leave his classroom and walk over to the rectory. He spotted me, and I asked if I could talk to him. I told him I wanted to apologize for what had happened. He told me to go away, that he didn't know what I was talking about.

"He kept walking, faster now, in front of me. I said, 'I'm going to tell my father what happened.' He stopped, turned quickly, and said, 'Come inside.'"

The rectory assistant, known to all the kids at St. Magnus as the "rectory rat", had earned that name years earlier.

She'd caught two boys smoking behind the dumpster and just happened to be driving by at the right (or wrong) time. The next day, she told the principal. Both kids got suspended.

The funny part? The principal ratted her out, told the boys exactly who had turned them in. From that day on, she wasn't Mrs. whatever anymore. She was just the rectory rat.

She said hello and asked Father if he wanted his "drink" in the study or his office. He told her to leave it in the study, then told me to meet him in his office.

Thomas's eyes drifted slightly upward. "I watched the assistant place a coffee cup on the desk in the study, her purse hanging from her wrist. She glanced at me with a raised eyebrow and walked out the front door."

"I rushed over to the cup and dumped the vial into it. I thought it was coffee, I was sure it would be coffee. But it was whiskey."

I turned and headed toward his office. Asher was already walking toward me. We met in the hallway.

"I thought I told you to wait in my office," he said through clenched teeth.

He was carrying a crumpled-up shirt and some other laundry. He brushed past me, grabbed the cup off the desk, and said, "Follow me."

We headed down the basement steps. I thought about pushing him, just one hard shove, but that wouldn't do the trick.

He walked over to the washing machine and dropped his dirty clothes on top, the cup still in his left hand. He took a sip, turned to face me, and pointed to a metal chair in the corner.

"Sit," he said, a command, not a request.

As he walked toward me, I started to stand, ready to bolt for the stairs. The rat had left. There was no one upstairs to shout to. No one to help.

He kept coming. When he got closer, he mumbled something I couldn't make out. Then he started shaking. His arms stretched out in front of him, stiff, like Frankenstein.

The cup was just inches from my face. I grabbed it from his hand.

He collapsed. Just dropped, like a sack of potatoes.

Thomas paused, looking down at the ground. "I ran up the stairs. That's when I saw you down the hallway. I closed the screen door behind me quietly. Didn't say anything. Just ran. I threw the cup in the dumpster as I passed St. Magnus."

He looked up at Dominic, voice low. "I must've dropped the empty vial in the basement."

"Now what?" Dom asked, raising his shoulders.

"The cops are gonna know he was poisoned!"

"Okay."

"Okay?!" Dominic hissed, his voice a sharp whisper. "You'll go to jail for murder!"

Thomas stared at him, unblinking. "You picked up the vial, Dom. You saved me."

Dominic froze.

"They ain't got nothin' but a dead priest in a basement. A dirty, dead priest that won't bother anyone anymore!" Thomas's voice rose, edged with something fierce and ragged. "We have to keep this buried. Like the bodies in this cemetery, Dom. Or we both go to jail."

Dominic's eyes darted down to the bottle again, then back up.

"You saw the body and didn't tell anyone. Right?"

Dom nodded slowly. "Yeah. Nobody knows."

His stomach twisted. Acid rose in his throat. He felt like throwing up.

"Was it murder?Anyone could've drunk that coffee. Thomas didn't know if it would kill a person; it was meant for dogs. Drinking it wasn't the same as injecting it… right?"

Dominic's mind scrambled, trying to justify it. Trying to unsee what he'd seen.

The two sat a moment longer, then slowly pedaled through the cemetery. It was cathartic, a way to erase the moment at hand. Their eyes scanned tombstones as they read names aloud. Memories surfaced with each turn: games of jailbreak, football on the grass, scraps that settled grudges, and the big oak tree where Dominic had his first kiss.

It wasn't Jasmine Dallas.

Saturday morning, Dominic slipped on his white Chuck Taylor high-tops and opened the front door.

"Priest of St. Magnus's Parish Found by Rectory Assistant"

The headline blared from the front page of the *Courier Post*, the newspaper folded neatly on Dominic's doorstep.

The article was short. No outpouring of grief. No quotes from mourning parishioners. Just murmurs like: *"He smoked a lot." "Never looked healthy."*

No one said, *"The parish will miss him."* Or *"A blow to the Christian community."*

Investigators told the press that Father Asher appeared to have suffered a heart attack or stroke, though that was just speculation. A full investigation would follow.

But no one mentioned poison.

No one mentioned a boy slipping out the back door.

No one suspected a thing.

By Monday, Asher's death was all the school could talk about. Rumors flew that he died doing laundry or hiding liquor in the basement.

But nothing about poisoning.

Nothing about Thomas.

Nothing about Dominic.

A week or so later, *The Star Herald* ran a story on Father Asher, a glowing piece, tucked between local council updates and a recipe for summer peach cobbler. The headline read: **"Beloved Clergyman Remembered for His Dedication to Youth."**

The article painted him as a pillar of the Catholic community. His warmth, his "unshakable faith," his "passion for teaching children the gospel" were all laid out like polished stones. A shepherd to the innocent. A teacher. A friend.

His obituary was even more succinct: *"Died of natural causes."*

But to Dominic, the line said something else entirely: no police investigation, nothing suspicious, no trace of poison in his body. No foul play.

Clean. Unquestioned. Tied up with a reverent bow.

Dominic stared at the paper for a long time, the weight of it pressing into his chest like a stone. The public saw a priest carried home by angels. He saw a monster gently lowered into the ground by silence, and protected, even in death, by the very institution that had once kept him untouchable.

The little foreign kid turned out to be Albanian. His name was Arben. His parents had died in a car accident, and he was now cared for by his grandparents, good people who had made their way out of Albania to raise their grandson.

They didn't have much and relied on help from anyone willing to give it. That's how Father Asher wormed his way in.

Gained their trust.

As if the boy hadn't suffered enough, now a holy man had taken full advantage of him. But after the death of Father Asher, whenever Dominic saw Arben at school, the kid was always smiling.

Once, he even saw them at the Summer festival, Arben and his grandparents, eating, laughing, and surrounded by newfound friends.

Father Asher's religion class that morning was taught by a lay teacher, Mrs. Hurley.

"Open your Bibles," she said. "The Book of Matthew."

Dominic flipped open his worn *Good News Bible*. One page was dog-eared, marked by a previous student. Underlined in pencil was a single verse, Matthew 18:6:

"If anyone causes one of these little ones, those who believe in me, to sin, it would be better for them to have a large millstone hung around their neck and to be drowned in the depths of the sea."

Dominic stared at the verse. He took his Bic ballpoint pen, uncapped it with his teeth, and traced over the faint pencil lines in blue ink. His hand trembled slightly.

He closed the Bible.

The summer passed like any other, hot days, wire-ball games in the middle of the street, two-hand touch football, lightning bugs, and spin-the-bottle parties with confiscated beer and whatever an older sibling was willing to share.

But for Dominic and Thomas, everything had changed.

They kept their pact and never spoke of Father Asher or the rectory basement again. Not once. In truth, they barely spoke at all after that.

Then, one day, Thomas was just gone, faded from the neighborhood without a word.

Thomas had always said his grandparents lived down the shore, and when they died, his family would inherit their house. When Dominic heard "shore," he automatically thought of Wildwood, New Jersey. So that became the assumption: Thomas had moved to Wildwood. Dominic figured his grandparents must have passed away by now, and that maybe Thomas lived there full-time.

Dominic and his father used to take day trips to Wildwood, long stretches of beach, fishing off the piers, strolling the boardwalk, and that ever-annoying tramcar voice creeping up from behind: "Watch the tramcar, please, watch the tramcar."

Dominic always thought he might run into Thomas someday. Every time he was down there, he looked for him, on the beach, in a crowded arcade.

That fall, high school began, ushering in a new life and a new set of friends. The past, like so much else in Dominic's world, was quietly boxed up and buried.

Four years flew by in a blink, adolescence, sports, acne, girls, SATs, and driving lessons with his Aunt "G", each one leaving its mark, then fading. A blur from the past, no matter how hard he tried to hold on, like some of the memories of his mother, kept alive not by him, but by the recollections of others.

After graduating from high school, he enrolled at Villanova. He was stunned when he received a four-year academic scholarship that covered most of his tuition, especially since his grades were average at best.

When the acceptance letter arrived, along with the scholarship notice, Jimmy simply smiled and said, "Nice."

As it turned out, their old friend Monsignor Cipolla was a regular at The Philly Tavern. Years of free Macallan, shared appetizers, and long talks about life and death, right and wrong, politics and religion had finally paid off. Inside that bar, they'd become closer than most.

Good bartenders know how to read a room, when to listen, when to pour a drink, when to offer a smile, and when to keep a secret. And "Jimmy D" had that gift.

Cipolla had his own kind of pull. Not like Jimmy's street-level hooks or knowing which state trooper to call to fix a ticket, Cipolla's connections ran deeper, stronger. His influence came through the Augustinians, who ran Villanova. One quiet call, no questions asked. Like Don Corleone in The Godfather: *Give this kid a scholarship.* Done. And that's where Dominic went.

During Dominic's time at Villanova, his father had taken ill and had to quit bartending at the Tavern. Stress, cigarettes, booze, and whatever else had been silently wreaking havoc inside him finally caught up with "Jimmy D." He never went to the doctor, so if there was anything he should've been managing, no one knew about it.

He passed away quietly in his sleep, not long after Dominic graduated from college.

The funeral was huge. Monsignor Cipolla, at the age of ninety, officiated the ceremony. Friends from Philly, family from Jersey, everyone showed up to celebrate Jimmy Di Angelo's life.

Dominic took it hard. For a while, he was lost in the grief. But thanks to his Aunt Gia, he found his footing again and managed to keep moving in the right direction.

Following in his father's footsteps, Dominic entered the Police Academy. Upon graduation, he was hired by the Camden County Police and spent the next twenty-four years trying to make a dent in the crime and decay of Camden City, a place barely nine square miles wide, yet long regarded as the most dangerous city in America.

And through it all, Dominic often thought of Thomas. Wondered where he'd ended up. If he had ever joined the military, like he always talked about.

Dominic recalled the times when Thomas came over as a kid. He'd stare at the Marine Corps emblem on Dominic's bedroom door.

"That's so cool," he used to say. "I'm joining the Marines someday."

Dominic never knew if he did.

Chapter 11

The teams were gathered in the squad room. Di Angelo stood at the front beside Entry Team Leader, Detective McKeown. McKeown was a veteran when it came to search warrants, kicking in doors, or locating fugitives on the run. He didn't just know his job, he lived it. Always putting his team first, always double-checking routes, gear, and safety. He was the kind of guy who should've been promoted years ago, but like so many others, he'd been overlooked by brass more interested in politics than performance, friends with less time on the job but more connections.

Di Angelo didn't mind that. Selfishly, a promotion would have pulled McKeown off his crew, and there wasn't anyone in the department who could do half the work with half the skill required. He didn't want his team breaching a door with someone green, someone untested. And for these early-morning hits, Di Angelo only wanted McKeown.

"Roll call," McKeown barked over the noise, gear clanking, Velcro ripping, quiet conversations laced with adrenaline, nerves, and caffeine. He held a clipboard in one hand, eyes scanning the room as he started down the list.

"Pumphrey."

"Here, sir."

"Pestridge."

"Here."

"McCaffrey."

"Here, sir."

"Michael John."

"Yo."

"Mugler."

"Yo yo."

"Phillips."

"Here."

"Malone, "

"He's on vacation," Sergeant Conners called out from the back, grinning. "Said to tell you, sir, he's here in spirit."

A few chuckles rose from the squad. McKeown didn't crack a smile. "Yeah, well, Malone's spirit seems to be here more than Malone lately."

"Another exotic vacation?" McKeown asked Conners.

"Of course!" The sergeant nodded, smiling. "He sent a text with a pic of him and three beautiful girls. They were sitting on a beach somewhere in Vaadhoo, Maldives. His text was one word, 'paradise.'"

McKeown just shook his head and called out a few more names, then the room settled. All eyes turned forward. It was getting close to game time.

Di Angelo stood beside the ops board, flipping through the warrant packet. He ran through the usual checklist, target details, layout of the house, potential threats, neighbouring structures, and entry points. His tone was crisp, confident. But he wasn't in tac gear like the others this time. No vest. No helmet. Just a dark suit and his badge clipped at the belt next to his holstered .40 calibre Glock. It was the look of a captain one would expect to find behind a desk, at a meeting, or in a press conference.

His team knew that look, and they didn't like it. When he wrapped up the briefing, he looked out at them.

"I wish I could be on the hit with you," he said. "But the brass upstairs has other ideas."

A few groans rolled through the room.

"From now on, I'm armchairing these hits from the office. Radio if I'm close. Cell if I'm not." He paused, letting that sink in. "But don't worry, breakfast after the raid is still non-negotiable. No one's taking that away."

That earned a few smirks and a nod from McKeown. Some things, at least, weren't changing in the minds of his detectives and sergeants. But they were.

Later that day, Di Angelo called a meeting with his top three detectives. As they entered the large smart room, they found him sitting at the head of the conference table, a coffee gone cold beside him and a thin folder unopened in front of him.

Silva pulled out a black high-back chair tucked under the mahogany table, collapsed into it, then leaned back, arms crossed. McKeown tapped a pen absently against his knee. Conners sat still, alert, like he already sensed what was coming.

Dominic cleared his throat. "I'm retiring," he said simply. "End of the year."

Silence fell upon the room. He let it hang there for a moment, like something sacred, or something shameful.

"A few months left. Then I'm gone. Someone else can run the show."

He didn't smile. Didn't soften the blow because there was no comfort in the truth, not for him, and not for the people in front of him.

They were his friends, brothers and sisters in arms. But he knew better than to offer them hope. They looked at each other, surprised but not shocked.

"Why? Who takes over? What the hell, Dom!" Silva said, her voice laced with disgust and bitterness.

Dominic shrugged. "Time for some bourbon and birds on my deck." He laughed softly. "I've got my wish list about who I'd like to take over."

In truth, he would be completely satisfied if any of the three got the spot. They were all worthy.

"Doesn't matter. Politics and stupidity will pick the next commander. I know you all know that." He leaned back in his chair, weary. "We still have some work to do. The commissioner wants to keep the Malmuth case open. Too many loose ends. James Hanlon is attempting to close any further investigations regarding our findings on his dead brother. I have no problem with that. However, Commissioner Scola wants homicide to keep it open because of the 'holy calling card' and a possible connection with the Malmuth case. I'll be the lead for a few more weeks on both cases. Child Protective Services will take over from there, handling interviews, providing counselling, and overseeing whatever else is needed in the matter of Stephanie Edmunds and her daughter's case."

Dominic had already signed off on the referral. The Hanlon family, too, would receive counselling. The county had protocols in place, a patchwork of trauma services and state-mandated programmes designed for families impacted by child sexual assaults. It wasn't perfect, but it was something.

"Whatever the county deems appropriate," Dominic had written in his final note on the case file. A bureaucratic phrase, maybe, but behind it there was genuine hope that someone, somewhere, might help these kids find their way back from what had been done to them.

Back when Dominic and his friend Thomas were kids, nothing like that existed, not publicly, anyway. No one ever said a word about priests, teachers, or anyone in a position of authority or guardianship molesting children. It wasn't until years later, when lawsuits piled up and victims seemed to fall out of trees, that the truth came out. The Church took a hit. So many paedophiles, under the guise of "Reverend," confessed to acts of molestation with their students or parishioners. So many cover-ups. The silence in the '60s and '70s had been deafening. Now it was impossible to ignore.

He looked at Conners. "Sarge, did we ever go back to Malmuth's to look for her cell again?"

"Not to my knowledge, sir. I can send a couple of agents over there today if you want."

"No. I'll stop by on my way home. It's not far from my house. I'll contact Cherry Hill PD and advise them that I need to get back in there. I'll be in touch, though."

"Okay, guys," Dominic said, pushing his chair back with a soft scrape. "That's all I needed to say. Let's get back to work."

McKeown stood first, nodding quietly. Silva followed, slower, watching Dominic a beat longer than necessary. As she reached the door behind McKeown, she paused just long enough to deliver the parting shot.

"You're such a jerk," she said over her shoulder, a crooked smirk playing at her lips.

Dominic smiled faintly. That was as close to affection as she got.

Only Conners remained, hands in his pockets, eyes lingering on the captain with something like admiration, or maybe resignation.

"Congrats, Cap," he said.

"We'll be fine. She'll be fine." He gestured vaguely, meaning the department. Or the unit. Or maybe something else entirely. "The task force, it'll fade into memory. Life here'll suck." He looked out the window facing the Delaware River. "Nice view up here. It's gonna suck without you, Cap. But we'll be fine."

He gave a stupid face like he was drunk or had been clocked by George Foreman's left hook and was about to go down for a ten count. They both laughed, a tired, knowing laughter that carried more truth than comfort.

Conners gave him a mock salute and turned for the door. Then he was gone, and the room was quiet again.

Dominic sat for a moment longer, staring at the empty chairs. The decision was made. The words were out. But something in his chest still felt unfinished. He reached into his suit jacket pocket, pulled out a set of keys, and headed out the door.

Di Angelo slowed as he turned down the street and into the Malmuth driveway. The yellow caution tape still flapped from the front door in the warm breeze, a silent, garish flag announcing tragedy to anyone curious enough to look.

He hated that crime scene tape. It gave everything away. It invited whispers, the kind that travelled fast down the unblemished sidewalks of Cherry Hill. Neighbours who leaned in too close, asked too many questions, and fancied themselves detectives because they pieced together scraps of gossip. The ones who would say, *"I knew he was up to no good,"* or, *"There was always something off about that house… too quiet."*

He stepped out of the car and tried the front door. Locked. He remembered what the witness, Jackie, had said, something about a spare key hidden out back under the cap of the deck railing. Worth a shot.

He made his way down the side of the house. The gates weren't locked, lucky. He was wearing a suit and didn't feel like climbing over. The large oak trees lining the property offered good cover, keeping him out of sight from any onlookers or cameras, assuming the neighbors even had any.

That was the thing about places like Cherry Hill. Upscale neighborhoods tended to breed a dangerous kind of naïveté. People lived in bubbles. They got too comfortable, untouched by reality. They couldn't imagine that bad things happened to good people. That walking down the streets in Camden could get you killed. That there were people out there who, if given the chance, would rob you blind, cut your throat, and move on with their day like nothing happened. And to them, it didn't.

Di Angelo hadn't walked the home's perimeter until now, and he could see how easy it would have been for someone to sneak up the long driveway and slip in through the back door. Jackie had probably mentioned that spare key under the deck rail one too many times.

Bad people were everywhere. And they counted on people like Jackie, people who assumed nothing bad would ever happen in areas like Cherry Hill. One wrong ear. One careless mistake. That was all it took to allow entry into the house.

He slipped through the backyard and located the key exactly where Jackie said it would be. The back door creaked open with a dry click.

Inside, the house felt… different. Warmer, almost unnaturally so. A stale, fruity stench hung in the air. He followed it to the kitchen, where the trash can lid stood open. Banana peels, or maybe some other rotting fruit, sat fermenting at the bottom. He tapped the sensor. The lid slid shut with a soft mechanical whirr.

Aside from that, the house was spotless. The crime scene team hadn't left their usual chaos behind. There were no overturned drawers, no stomped-out carpet. Impressive. Or suspicious.

Di Angelo pulled on a pair of black latex gloves and began to search, hands slipping under cushions, behind the sofa, beneath furniture, anywhere a phone could have been missed in a rush. Nothing.

He moved through the living room, scanning. That's when he noticed the door to the garage. It was ajar. A shadow moved beyond it.

Di Angelo's pulse ticked up. He dropped into a quiet stance, drew his weapon, and crept forward. As he reached the door, he spotted a narrow mirror tucked into a wall alcove. Maybe it was just a trick of the light, a reflection. Still, he didn't take chances.

He kicked the door open hard. "Police! Who's in here?"

Silence.

He stepped inside. Again: "Police! Show yourself!"

Still nothing. The garage smelled of motor oil and old wood. A white Range Rover sat in the centre bay, its windows down.

He moved alongside it and glanced in. There it was, Judy Malmuth's phone, sitting on the driver's seat like a gift.

"What the hell…" he muttered. "Horrible search, guys."

He scanned the space again, then finally holstered his weapon.

Reaching in, he opened the Rover's door and slid into the driver's seat. The leather was warm. The remote sat in the middle console cup holder. He picked up the phone. It was dead.

And then a voice, low and close.

"Dominic."

Di Angelo inhaled sharply, twisting toward the sound, hand already reaching for his gun. A figure shifted in the back seat.

"It's Thomas. Thomas Hawk."

Dominic froze, hand still near his holster, but didn't turn. He could see the man clearly enough in the rearview mirror. Older, yes, but unmistakable, the same slicked-back waves of hair, the same eyes, that same voice. East Coast, North Jersey, or New York, maybe. It hadn't changed at all.

"Dude," Dominic said, trying to steady his breathing. "What the hell, man? What are you doing here? How'd you get in?"

Thomas smiled, perfectly calm. "Didn't mean to scare you, Dom. Big-time captain now, huh? You got in. So did I."

He chuckled, soft and dry. "I've followed your career over the years. Knew you were one of the good ones. Knew you'd make the Merchant Street crew proud. Your old man would've been proud, too. Sorry about your pop, by the way. He was cool as shit."

"Yeah. He was." Dominic's patience was wearing thin. "I could've killed you."

"But you didn't."

"Get out of the car, Thomas!"

"Wait," Thomas said. "I knew Judy Malmuth."

That stopped Dominic. He took his hand off the door handle and settled back in the seat. "And?"

"She called me. Wanted me to take care of Marvin."

"What do you mean by 'take care of'?"

Thomas gave him a sideways glance. "You've seen enough gangster movies, Dom."

"Did you?"

"Yes. Well… not exactly." He stretched out his arms, relaxed. Miss Judy did the deed. She wanted him dead. Said she'd inherit everything, insurance, assets, all in her name. She made sure of that. Anyway, remember the poison I used on Father Asher? The dog stuff? Suxamethonium chloride. Turns out it's untraceable. Just a couple of drops in someone's system, and it's gone within thirty minutes, no trace left behind. A toxicologist's nightmare."

He grinned. "Gotta love the internet. Instant knowledge at your fingertips. Back when I did Asher, we didn't have that luxury. I worried about them finding out for years. I worried if you would tell anyone, too."

Dominic stared ahead, jaw clenched. "Even knowing that piece of shit molested a young kid and tried to molest me, you still never wavered on your Catholic faith and the church. Befriending priests and goin to Villanova…"

Thomas shook his head, disappointment etched across his face.

"You can't play God, Thomas! Asher was a pedophile, but not all

154

priests fall into that category. Just like with cops. Some are crooked, sure, but it doesn't mean we all are."

Thomas leaned forward, closer to the front seat. Their eyes locked in the rearview mirror, rage meeting rage, burning into each other's retinas.

"Tell that to the victims. To the parents of all the kids the Malmuths defiled."

Di Angelo dropped his gaze from the mirror. Thomas had a point, somewhere in the storm of his rage, but he also knew vigilantism wasn't the answer. And deep down, he feared it was only a matter of time before Thomas got caught.

"How did Judy know what to do with the poison?" Di Angelo asked.

"I showed her how to use it," Thomas continued. "We met up a few times at the 541. Your old hangout back in the day. I showed her how to load a syringe from the vial and exactly how much to fire into her hubby's mug of hot coffee. *Just a few drops does the trick,* I told her."

We practiced on the coffee cups at the diner. I gave her a few more tips, you know, how to clean up, erase her prints, and tidy up the place after the deed was done. She followed instructions to a T. No mistakes. Natural killer." He paused, then added, "Of course, it's easier when you hate someone so much. She hated Marvin. Knew what he was doing with those girls. Knew for years. Kept quiet about it, though. At first, she only watched. Until she realized how much easier things would be if she got involved. That's when she confronted him about the child porn, the trading, the dark web. But instead of divorcing him or turning him in, she chose complicity. It started small. Covering his tracks with the Edmunds kid. Keeping Marvin out of sight. She convinced herself that if she was involved, the girls wouldn't really be violated, just posed like they were. Just pictures. Then those images would be sold on the dark web for a lot of money. Easy money. She justified it. Told herself it wasn't as bad as it looked. Besides, she hated Stephanie Edmunds. Feared she was getting too close to Marvin's money. That he'd leave everything to her, Judy didn't want her getting a single dime of Marvin's small fortune. Judy was playing Marvin. The Marvins played Stephanie and a dozen others. But I played Judy. I'll admit, I was a little shocked the first time I followed her to the Whitman Hotel. That's where they had the room. That's where the filming happened. The photoshoots. The drugging and the molestation of little girls, unaware of what was happening to them. That's where innocence went to die. I surveilled the hotel one weekend and watched girls go in and out. Young, beautiful girls from about 11 to 14, maybe 15 years old. Judy was the transporter and bullshit agent. It was apparent that she had built trust with them. Hell, she greeted the parents sometimes as they would drop them off, all under the illusion of a modeling deal. She had the look and the charisma to sell it. The parents believed her. They wanted to believe her. That's what made the con so easy." Especially the desperate ones, poor families without the means to build portfolios or pay for shoots. Sure, she gave them a few nice photos to keep up with the charade. Only needed one session. They'd drug the kids, strip them, molest them, and pose them. With Marvin's grotesque body all over them while, Judy snapped the shots. Shots that sick perverts requested and paid high prices for. When they woke from the drug-induced sleep, Judy would say, "Oh, honey, you passed out," or ask what happened, slipping in questions like *What did you eat today?*, acting concerned, playing dumb. Then she'd spin it for the parents: "She got sick, probably the heat or nerves. Happens all the time with kids."

Meanwhile, the child had no idea. No memory. Just a vague sense that something was off. All they believed happened was that they were taking headshots and then blacked out. Judy was a decent photographer. The proof was there, a few nice photos and a cheap portfolio, but no modelling contract. No callbacks. Just confusion.

But what they didn't get, what they never saw or could imagine, was their child, drugged into unconsciousness after drinking from a tampered water bottle. One sip, and everything after that went black.

Holly was the low-hanging fruit, a bonus that came with his mistress. Thomas' eyes darkened. But Judy finally got her revenge.

"The day she killed her husband, she didn't show any signs of remorse or worry about facing her friend Jackie, or anyone, for that matter. Kill the guy and head off to yoga like it was nothing. That's when I met her in the driveway as she was pulling out. She was nervous, but she trusted me. I told her to pull back in.

"She did. She parked, right here. I closed the garage door. She got out of the car. I walked up to her, wrapped an arm around her waist, and slipped the needle into the small of her back. A smooth push, two cc's of dog poison, just under the skin. She gave a tiny little flinch. I saw it in her eyes. The needle hit right in the middle of that colorful butterfly tattoo, a regretted tramp stamp, no doubt. So many colors, great for hiding a tiny needle puncture."

Dominic felt his pulse spike.

"She went down fast. I carried her to the bedroom, undressed her quickly, before death stole all the life from her toned body. Then I laid her in bed. Thought about making it look like a suicide, a bottle of sleeping pills, or a hypodermic next to her with an open bag. It would've been easy to inject her before our dog poison fully kicked in. Then I changed my mind. Still, I left some heroin laced with fentanyl on the nightstand. Just enough to muddy the waters. She was too fit to be a junkie, but I thought it might buy me time. Take your good detectives down the wrong path for a few days."

"Why the laptop?" Di Angelo asked quietly, still facing down, listening to this madman.

"I was going to leave my calling card," Thomas said with a grin. "But the laptop was sitting right there on the dresser. So I figured, why not? Left a little note, Matthew 18:6. You know the one."

He smiled wider. "It's your favorite verse. For good reason."

"That's why you highlight it on every child porn bust, Dom. Because deep down, you know, these people deserve to drown for what they've done. The Malmuths, Hanlon, and all the rest. Thomas gave a short laugh through his nose as he shook his head. Hanlon said I didn't look like a therapist. Asshole was right. He was a sick monster, too. They're all sick monsters. Nobody was going to keep these people behind bars or punish them for what they'd done to these children! That's why I left the Malmuths with the sounds of that little girl's voice being raped by her own father. Made sure it was the last thing they would hear as their souls entered hell."

He looked Dominic straight in the eyes, his voice eerily calm. "'Better a millstone be tied around your neck and drowned in the sea.' I'm your millstone, Dom."

Di Angelo took a slow, steadying breath and leaned forward in the seat, his body tensing. He shifted slightly to his right, fingers wrapping around the grip of his holstered Glock.

"What are you thinking, Dom? Turn me in? Take the chance of me telling them everything I know about you? All the years of keeping quiet about the death of a priest?"

Thomas sat back, arms folded across his chest.

"They won't believe you," Di Angelo said in a matter-of-fact tone.

"So what! It's news that will get your reputation tarnished. Your family will be brought into the limelight. Attention you don't want or need," Thomas said, driving his point home.

Di Angelo eased his grip on the gun. With his left hand, he pressed the garage door remote clipped to the visor.

The door creaked open, its slow rise echoing like a countdown.

"Get out. Go away," he said, low but firm.

Thomas smiled. "That's my pal Dom. I knew you were still in there somewhere."

He pulled the handle, popped the latch, and slipped out of the car without a sound. Leaning into the door, he closed it gently as he disappeared into the early evening dusk.

Di Angelo sat frozen, hands trembling on the wheel. He reached up and pressed the remote again. The door began its noisy descent. His head throbbed with rage, guilt, and confusion, tormented by the decision he had just made: to let Thomas go… or take the only other option. Kill him.

"Cap?"

A voice shot across the garage bay. It was McKeown. Sergeant Conners had told him to drive by the Malmuths' and meet Di Angelo there. He entered through the back door, the same one Di Angelo had kicked open moments ago.

"Is that you, Cap?" McKeown yelled from the doorway, his gun low at the ready, just as the motion sensor clicked on the garage lights.

Di Angelo didn't respond. He was still in a dazed state behind the wheel.

Puzzled by what he was seeing, McKeown moved slowly and

tactically toward the Range Rover, raising his weapon until the sights met his eyes. He scanned his gun over the vehicle, yelling, "Hands! Let me see your hands!"

Di Angelo heard the command and was pulled from his deep thoughts. He raised his hand quickly.

"McKeown! It's me. Don't shoot, brother!"

"Fuckin' A, Cap!" McKeown exhaled sharply, lowering his weapon. "I almost blew your damn head off."

He holstered his gun and leaned on the fender of the vehicle, rubbing his forehead. "What the hell are you doing inside that vehicle?"

Di Angelo glanced into the rearview mirror. The garage door was completely down. Thomas was gone. Not a shadow. Not a whisper. Just empty rear seats.

"I was double-checking for Judy Malmuth's cell. Just got thinking about the case and started drifting off, I guess." Di Angelo's hands were trembling slightly. "Damn. I'm losing it."

"You need some rest, Cap." McKeown gave him a tired smile. "And I need a drink. That was nuts," he said with a sigh of relief that he hadn't pulled the trigger on his captain, his friend.

"Yeah. Crazy," Di Angelo said, his voice quieter now, unsteady.

McKeown glanced around the dim garage, then poked his head into the Rover. He opened the back door.

Di Angelo tensed. Had Thomas left something behind? A clue? A scent? Anything that might trigger suspicion?

"Car looks brand new back here," McKeown said, inspecting casually. "Guess this is what a back seat looks like when there's no kids to carpool around." He held up a baseball cap. "Look at this!"

Di Angelo's nerves snapped tight. He twisted in his seat to face him.

"Not one Cheerio lodged between the seats!" McKeown added with a snort.

Di Angelo forced a laugh, sharp and awkward.

"Any sign of Mrs. Malmuth's cell?" McKeown asked.

Di Angelo was still in the front seat, Judy Malmuth's phone wedged between his thighs. "No. Nothing," he said. "I checked everywhere. Let's get out of here."

"Roger that, Cap."

Di Angelo stepped out of the Rover and followed McKeown through the open door leading into the house. The two had worked side by side for over a decade, riding patrol together, running deep in undercover narcotics and vice. They had kicked in hundreds of doors, seen the worst of the city shoulder to shoulder. And unlike most people Di Angelo worked with, McKeown had earned a place in his personal life too.

Di Angelo's gut churned with guilt as they stepped out of the house. He couldn't believe he had just lied to the one person he trusted most, and who trusted him just as deeply.

He had broken the brotherhood code. Lied straight to his face. Hid evidence. It didn't sit right.

What the hell is Thomas doing? he thought, slipping the key back beneath the deck railing cap.

But he had no choice. He had to keep the past hidden, the past that had taken him years to cope with.

To justify in his mind that it was ok to keep Thomas Hawk's identity a secret. Di Angelo drove home with Judy's cell resting in his jacket pocket. When he entered the house, he placed her phone on the charger beside his recliner in the living room. Ann never used that one; she preferred the kitchen outlet and probably wouldn't notice. Even though the phone was red, not black like his, it might blend in.

He watched as the green lightning bolt appeared on the screen. *Charging.* Beneath it: *0%.* And under that: *2.5 hours until full charge.* The data warrant had expired, so there was no risk of it pinging the office.

He sank into the leather sofa, eyes fixed on the phone. What was he going to find on it? And more importantly, what would he do with it? He couldn't turn it in now. He had already told McKeown he didn't find anything. Maybe he could sneak it back into Malmuth's house. But returning there risked being seen.

He exhaled hard, closed his eyes, and pulled the recliner lever. The footrest popped up, the chair embracing his tired frame. He lay still, but his mind raced until mental exhaustion won, and he fell into a deep sleep.

Ann dimmed the lights, watching her husband drift off from the other room.

About an hour later, the sound of voices stirred Di Angelo from his slumber. He recognized one of them, Ann. She was in the kitchen, talking and laughing with someone. Then he heard her say, "Gemma."

Relief settled over him. Their daughter was on the phone. Ann was laughing, so it wasn't bad news, not a sickness, not a crime. Still, his mind had already traveled the dark road it always did. That was the reflex now. Whenever Gemma's name lit up on his phone or she called her mother at an odd hour, his gut tightened. Never once did he think, *Oh, good, Gemma, maybe she has some great news.*

No. His thoughts always turned to *Who's dead? Who's in jail? What happened?* Years of chasing darkness had twisted him that way. And worst of all, he knew it had twisted Ann, too.

Once Judy Malmuth's phone's screen lit up, he went straight to the photos. Nothing jumped out, no obvious incriminating shots. He moved on to the messages. One name stood out: *Hawk.*

He opened the thread. The texts were numerous but brief. Short questions. Short answers. Cold. Cryptic. Like two people in on something they didn't want written down.

Next to the name *Hawk* in the text thread, Di Angelo tapped the phone icon and raised Judy's cell to his ear. It rang once. Twice. Then, he felt a tap on his shoulder.

Startled, he jumped. Ann stood behind him, holding out his personal phone. "Sorry, I didn't mean to scare you." She whispered. "Your phone was buzzing," "It says 'Private Caller.'"

Di Angelo quickly ended the call on Judy's cell and took his phone from Ann. As she turned back toward the kitchen, she called over her shoulder, "Gemma says hi, hun."

Di Angelo looked down; his own screen was dark now. Whoever had called had hung up. He glanced back at Judy's phone. The screen was also black.

The connection was broken on both ends.

Chapter 12

The room was packed, law enforcement officers in uniform, prosecutors and detectives in sharp suits, and a scattering of civilians, all gathered to say goodbye. Up front sat Ann, her hands neatly folded in her lap, with Gemma beside her. John, their son-in-law, sat to the left of Dominic, and to his right was Aunt "G," who stared straight ahead, her expression unreadable.

Commissioner Scola stood at the podium, delivering her farewell tribute. Her voice carried through the space, steady and sincere, as she recited accolade after accolade. She called Dominic a cornerstone of the department, a visionary who had ushered them into the tech era and a relentless force in the pursuit of justice.

Dominic didn't necessarily disagree with his friend and secret confidant in the office, but he hated the spotlight. Always had. He would have preferred to skip the whole thing, meet up at The Victory with a few trusted faces, toss some darts, and chase down a few beers. That was more his speed. But Ann would have killed him if he had bailed on this.

She had always believed that when Dominic took the oath to serve, she had been drafted too. She had walked beside him through the long nights, the sudden calls, the days he spent holed up undercover in ratty apartments, dingy motels, even sleeping in his car during endless surveillance runs. He would sneak calls to her just to say he was okay.

And she was always there, waiting for the sound of the front door opening, the clink of his keys landing on the foyer table.

She could tell when the job had followed him home, when the silence said more than words ever could. Because of all the sacrifices they had made, all they had endured together, she insisted he accept every bit of recognition that came his way. Even if it was just a county luncheon with lukewarm food and cut-up hoagies, she wanted him to take the praise. He had earned it. And so had she.

Now, it was his turn to speak. He stood, adjusted the buttons on his jacket, and made his way to the podium. He had written something the night before, a proper speech, full of thanks and nods to the past. But, true to form, he had left it on the kitchen table, right next to his coffee mug and reading glasses.

He had planned to read it. Thank everyone publicly. Keep it simple. Deliver it with passion and pride. Then, sit back down and have some lunch. Instead, he looked out at the crowd, his family, his colleagues, his ghosts, and decided to wing it.

Dominic spoke from the heart. He mentioned a few key events, some of the darker ones that had shaped him, some of the lighter ones that had kept him grounded. He thanked the brass by name, but only the ones who had earned it in his eyes. The rest? Well, they already knew where they stood with him. There was no pretending in Dominic Di Angelo's world, and he wasn't about to start now.

He thanked his detectives, most of all the ones who went through hell beside him, who kicked down doors and dug through the worst humanity had to offer.

"These officers and detectives," he said, his voice firm, "are the first defense against the heinous crimes committed against our children."

A few heads nodded; some glanced down, humbled.

He turned to his family. He thanked Ann and Gemma for their patience and sacrifice over twenty-five years. They had adjusted to his long nights and missing holidays, to the man who came home with too many secrets and not enough sleep.

But it was when he spoke about Aunt Gia that his voice nearly gave out. He paused, took a breath.

"To my Aunt G," he said, "she helped my dad raise me, she helped me to succeed, and made sure I got what other kids in the neighborhood got when birthdays or Christmas came around, even if it came a little later."

He smiled and looked at his aunt. "I lost my mother at a very early age," he said, his tone touched with sadness and regret, "and my Aunt "G" , Doctor Giavanna Di Angelo, did her best to fill that void. She made sure I never missed school events, like the prom or the school trip to Hershey Park. She helped with school projects and college papers."

"She took me on countless trips to the Philadelphia Zoo, where we studied the differences between male and female animals of every species. It became our monthly ritual. For those of you who haven't guessed, my aunt is a retired veterinarian. She was my first boss at my first job, at The Penn Dog Shelter, caring for sick and lonely dogs. She taught me how to comfort them and make their last days as peaceful as possible."

"And when I lost my dad, she stepped up again. She was the first one I showed when I bought my wife's engagement ring. She was there for my screw-ups, and she was there when I got it right."

He blinked hard and kept going, barely holding it together. "She believed in me when I didn't believe in myself. Thank you, Aunt G."

The room stood as he finished. A wall of applause erupted around him, tight-gripped handshakes, hugs from people who had shared trenches with him, and a few from those who just wanted to be near his gravity for a moment longer.

Later, at one of the luncheon tables, Aunt Gia sat beside Gemma. Across the room, Dominic, Ann, and Gemma's husband, John, were laughing quietly in the buffet line.

Gia leaned in. "Aren't you proud of your father?" she asked.

Gemma smiled. "Absolutely. He's an incredible father. If I could be even half the person he is, I'd be grateful. I know he's not perfect, and we've had our moments. But no matter how rough things got between us, I always knew he'd do whatever he could to be there for me… or die trying."

Gemma stared across at her father with admiration, listening as his detectives and friends shared stories from the field, stories he would have never told her himself. She was hearing things now that she wished she'd known sooner. Though he had shared a few gruesome tales, about bodies pulled from the Delaware River, and heartbreaking ones, like the boy who asked, *"Am I going to die?"* after being shot in the belly, then died in his arms, these stories she overheard were different. They were fuller, rich with details.

She looked at her Aunt Gia and said, "All I want for him now is to slow down. To rest. To sit with me and watch the hawks circling the sky, like we used to when I was a child. He could spot one and name it in a second. *'That's a Red-tail… no, wait, that's a Cooper's. Or maybe a Northern.'* He loves those birds. Honestly, I think they helped keep him sane through the years."

She paused for a moment, then laughed softly as she placed her hand over her aunt's. "That… and a little bourbon."

She chuckled at the memory, eyes glassy with something between sadness and affection.

Gia nodded, warmth in her expression. "You remind me of him sometimes. He's done so much. Sometimes I can't believe that little boy, always tearing through the neighborhood, getting into everything, is the same man up there today."

She touched her chest, her voice dipping a little softer. "He used to be a bit of a loner, and that used to kill me. Watching him ride his bike alone, play by himself in the yard… And when he got scared or really mad, he had this little imaginary friend. What did he call him? *Thomas,* I think. Yes, he called him Thomas."

Gemma's brow creased slightly. "My Dad had an imaginary friend named Thomas? That's funny."

"He never told you about that?" Aunt Gia asked.

"No."

"Yeah. I don't know where he came up with the name *Thomas,* but when I would ask him who he was talking to, he would always say, 'Thomas.' He used to set up a little pillow next to his in bed. He'd talk to him, laugh with him. It was cute. Sweet, really. Then he got older and made real friends, and Thomas faded away, I guess."

Gia's gaze drifted across the room again. Dominic caught her watching him. His eyes, now creased with age at the corners, still radiated that sharp, unmistakable blue. He smiled, a quiet warmth behind it. Gia smiled back, though something in her chest tightened as she watched him.

So many years. So many secrets.

"God, may he finally find peace of mind and enjoy his retirement with his wife and family," she whispered, a small prayer, her eyes closing for just a moment.

Chapter 13

The U-Haul was packed to the roof, boxes wedged and strapped into every corner like a tight game of Tetris. Dominic slapped the side of the truck and grinned.

"Ann, we're gonna need a bigger boat," he said, stealing his favorite line from *Jaws*, something he'd repeated far too many times over the years.

Ann was in her car. His Audi, freshly waxed so the jet-black finish gleamed like a diamond, was hitched to the U-Haul and ready for takeoff. She rolled her eyes playfully as she watched him climb into the driver's seat of the truck.

"Pittsburgh, here we come," Dominic said with a grin, putting the truck in drive. "We're gonna be Yinz's now, Primanti Brother's sandwiches and all."

His phone buzzed just as he started down the road.

He had handed in the work cell. For the first time in decades, the buzzing of a cell phone didn't rattle him. His old ringtone, once a trigger that yanked him out of sleep, away from holidays, dinners, and moments with family, was now just another sound in the world. He still felt the jolt sometimes when he heard the same tone coming from someone else's phone. A flicker of anxiety. But it was fading. With enough time and distance from the job, he hoped it would vanish altogether.

The phone buzzed again. This time, he answered it with a smile, never even looking at the caller's name or number.

"Hello."

"Hey, it's Damon." The voice on the other end was calm, as if they spoke often. "I got another one… if you're interested."

There was a long pause, a beat where the smile faded from Dominic's face, replaced by something else. Something from his past, maybe. Yet it felt very familiar.

He gripped the steering wheel tight and looked straight ahead, out toward the open road, with his cell pressed against his ear. The hum of the U-Haul's tires rolling over I-76 filled the silence in the cab as he listened, expressionless.

Then he said, flatly, "Retired," and ended the call.

He tossed the cell onto the passenger seat. Just then, Ann pulled alongside him in her car. Dominic glanced over at her from his driver's side window and smiled. He gave her a thumbs-up as she sped ahead. They had agreed to meet at Sidling Hill Rest Stop for a bite, neutral ground, halfway to their new chapter in life.

Dom took in a deep breath and exhaled like a man about to free dive. His fingers tightened around the wheel, knuckles pale against the black leather. His eyes flicked to the silenced cell on the passenger seat, then back to the road, again and again.

"Retired," he muttered. "Retired, indeed."

The word felt like a joke, like something other men got to be.

A few miles passed. The highway stretched out, empty and humming beneath the tires. Finally, he reached over, grabbed the phone, and checked the recent call.

Life Gym and Spa, and the number.

He hit send.

Two rings, then a male voice answered. "Damon, Life Gym and Spa, how can I help you?"

The voice on the other end sounded familiar somehow. A strange comfort settled over him, like slipping into an old coat, worn and frayed, but still warm.

Di Angelo's voice responded, low and steady.

"What do ya got?"

The End.

www.ingramcontent.com/pod-product-compliance
Lightning Source LLC
Chambersburg PA
CBHW040824010826
48978CB00012BB/607